Out of the Storm

PATRICIA WILLIS grew up on a farm in the hills of eastern Ohio. She studied geography at Ohio University and Kent State University and is an avid student of American History, particularly the Civil War. With her husband and two sons, she has explored historic sites throughout the country. Ms. Willis lives in North Canton, Ohio.

Out of the Storm

PATRICIA WILLIS

AN AVON CAMELOT BOOK

For Bill Jr., Matthew, and Wesley,
who add a special sparkle to the world.

AVON BOOKS
A division of
The Hearst Corporation
1350 Avenue of the Americas
New York, New York 10019

First Avon Camelot Printing: November 1996

CAMELOT TRADEMARK REG. U.S. PAT. OFF. AND IN OTHER COUNTRIES, MARCA REGISTRADA,
HECHO EN U.S.A.

Printed in the U.S.A.

OPM 10 9 8 7 6 5 4 3 2

chapter ❧ one

Mandy slipped into the kitchen chair, eyeing the platter of steaming chicken. Being late to supper was her way of letting everyone know she didn't like this place. But she might have come sooner if she'd known they were having fried chicken.

"We'll try to have supper at six every evening, if that suits everybody," Aunt Bess stated.

Mandy's eyes slid away from her great-aunt's stern gaze. From the moment they'd arrived, Aunt Bess had been bossing everyone, telling them where to put things, warning them not to scratch the woodwork. Now that they were moved in, Mandy felt as if a trapdoor had slammed shut behind her. The farm was a prison and Aunt Bess the warden. There was nothing to look forward to now except leaving, and August was months away.

"The store closes at seven in the evenings," Mandy's mother said to Aunt Bess, "so I should be home shortly after that. But Mandy and Ira will be here at six."

Aunt Bess nodded. "I'll keep some supper warm for you." She took a sip of water. "It's been a long time since I cooked for anyone but myself. Do you remember, Vera, when you came and stayed with me years ago?"

"Yes, I do. It was the summer I turned fourteen."

Mandy saw her mother glance around the kitchen, perhaps trying to recall how it had looked when she was a girl.

"I don't think you've been back here since you married," Aunt Bess said. "I'm so glad you stopped in last month."

"So am I. It was good to come back. And to get the job with Mr. Armstrong too."

"I'm sure he's pleased to find someone with experience," Aunt Bess said. "And I'm pleased you're here with me," she added.

She's not pleased I'm here, Mandy mused; she hasn't said one word to me yet. Shutting out the table talk, Mandy let her thoughts spin back across time, stirring up the dust of the past unhappy weeks. When her mother had lost her job at the grocery store to a returning war veteran, she'd been unable to find any other work in Garnet Creek. Her job hunting took her to the surrounding towns and the visit with Aunt Bess.

Mandy frowned, recalling the day her mother had announced they were moving to Parrish Grove. She'd never forgive her mother for making them leave their home. Garnet Creek was only forty miles away but it seemed like a thousand.

"You've grown, Ira, since I saw you last summer at the reunion," Aunt Bess was saying.

"I know." Ira grinned. "Just like a bad weed."

"You shouldn't have any trouble keeping the woodbox filled," Aunt Bess said, smiling back.

"That's right," Vera said. "We're grateful for a place to stay, Aunt Bess, and we want to help you all we can."

"The sheep are the most work," Aunt Bess said. "I've decided to give Mandy the job of bringing them in to the barn every day."

Mandy's head jerked up. She hadn't paid much attention when her mother told her and Ira about Aunt Bess's sheep. Now the thought of going out in the pasture field with the strange animals scared Mandy. She wished Aunt Bess had given the chore to Ira instead of her, but she guessed since she was twelve and Ira only nine, she was the logical choice.

"I don't know anything about sheep," she murmured.

"There's nothing much to know about them," Aunt Bess said. "They just have to be brought in at night and fed." She went on to explain that a mother sheep was a ewe, pronounced "you," and the female sheep not yet old enough to have lambs were called yearlings. "If you don't think you can do it . . ." Aunt Bess's voice trailed off.

"Of course she can do it!" Mandy's mother spoke up. "Do they need to be brought in now?"

"No, they're already in the barn," Aunt Bess said.

The talk of sheep had made Mandy lose all desire for supper. "I think I'll go outside and look around," she said, sliding out of her chair.

"It's getting dark," her mother said, studying Mandy with a frowning gaze.

"I'm not afraid of the dark," Mandy muttered and hurried toward the back door.

"She has her father's eyes," Mandy heard Aunt Bess say as she stepped out into the cold night. A bitterness welled up in her that she could almost taste. What right did Aunt Bess have to speak of her father as if he were just off at work or something? She should know they wouldn't want to talk about him. Mandy swallowed hard. The months ahead were going to be even worse than she'd imagined.

In the darkness, she could barely see the shadowy front porch. When she finally had to accept that they were moving in with Aunt Bess, she'd hoped the house would have a big porch. In fact, on the way over in the truck today, she'd crossed her fingers and repeated over and over to herself, "It has a front porch, it has a front porch, it has a front porch."

The moment Mandy had seen the front porch, she knew it was never used. The sandstone steps were almost hidden beneath clumps of untrimmed shrubs. A wrought iron railing along the outer

4

porch edge stood bent and rusting, the skeleton of a dead vine still clinging to it. The porch was cluttered with junk, a broken chair, some dead potted plants, a stack of bricks. Brown leaves, shifting in every stir of air, rattled along the porch floor and climbed up the corner by the door.

Seeing the porch there in the darkness reminded Mandy of her father. Time and again he'd said that every house should have a big front porch. He'd claimed there was no better place to visit, to shell peas, to rest after a long day's work. He'd told her and Ira it was the perfect place to enjoy a summer storm. If it were raining this very minute, Mandy thought, Aunt Bess's porch would be the last place I'd go to get out of the storm.

When the cold finally chased her inside, she bypassed the kitchen and went straight to her room. She struck a match and lit the oil lamp on the dresser. The warm, flickering light brightened the room that she still couldn't think of as hers.

She frowned at herself in the dresser mirror, pulling on the single braid hanging like a thick rope down her back. Aunt Bess had said that she had her father's eyes. Mandy leaned closer to the mirror. Were her father's eyes brown too? She couldn't remember. At that moment, she couldn't remember her father's face at all.

Just then, her mother came into the room and dropped down on the bed. She began pulling hairpins from the coiled knot of hair at the back of her head. "Mandy, I'll need you and Ira at the store tomorrow. I'll be going down early, but you can sleep in awhile. The store's only a half a mile or so down the county road."

Mandy nodded. Tomorrow was Saturday, and she and Ira had already made plans to go down and look over the store. It was probably like any other country store, cluttered, dusty, with the mixed odors of cheese and turpentine and stale tobacco, and a mustiness that always made Mandy want to sneeze. She wondered if Mr. Armstrong would be there. She'd never met him but she knew all about him. He was sick and had hired her mother to manage the store until he was well again. He planned to have an operation soon, then recuperate over the summer and be back to work by fall. Mandy knew all that, but it didn't make her feel any better about living here.

"Mandy, I want you to be on time for meals. Aunt Bess has been good enough to let us move in here until the fall. We don't want to be a burden to her."

The resentment Mandy had been holding inside came pouring out. "I don't want to live here, Mama. Everything's so strange, and Aunt Bess doesn't like me."

"Oh, Mandy, she just doesn't know you yet. She's a fine person . . ."

"I wish summer was over and we could go home."

"This is the only home we've got right now, Mandy."

"This will never be home," Mandy said, pulling her braid over her shoulder and holding it against her cheek. "Why did we have to leave Garnet Creek?"

"We've been over this before," her mother said, drawing in a deep breath before she continued. "I would've liked to stay in Mr. Fettering's bungalow, but when he raised the rent, we just couldn't afford it anymore."

"We could've moved in with Grandma Gates," Mandy said.

"I won't take charity, Mandy, and you know I couldn't find any work in Garnet Creek. Besides, Grandma Gates's house is too small for four people."

"What about the money we've saved? I thought we were going to buy the Fulton place. Remember, Mama, how much Dad wanted to . . ."

"Mandy!" Her mother's voice was sharp and cold, like steel cutting ice.

Ignoring the warning tone, Mandy went on. "He dreamed of living in the Fulton place. All of us did."

"Mandy, that's all over now."

"It can't be over. We have to get the Fulton place . . . we have to!" Mandy paused over a new thought. "Maybe Mrs. Fulton would let us move in with her when your job is finished here."

Her mother sighed and stood up. "I just can't

think about that now," she said. She moved toward the doorway, then stopped to look back at Mandy. "We don't always get what we want in life, Mandy." A moment later she was gone.

Mandy got up and jerked open a dresser drawer, muttering under her breath, "That's the truth!" Then she saw the money in the bottom of the drawer, seven five-dollar bills. Each month her father was away in the war, he'd sent her five dollars and told her to save it for the Fulton place.

Mandy picked up the bills, holding them as she imagined her father had once held them in his own hands. Some faded and tattered, some crisp and new, they always reminded her of the Fulton place. Even now, the familiar image rose in her mind, comforting and painful at the same time. With its broad front porch and sheltering trees, the house beckoned, cool and white and waiting.

As clearly as if it were yesterday, she remembered the day she and her father and Ira had gone to the Fulton place to cut down a dead tree. When Mrs. Fulton talked about selling the property, Mandy's father had asked if he could have first chance to buy it. Being an old friend, Mrs. Fulton had readily agreed, though she told him she didn't know just when she would put it up for sale.

Mandy could still hear her father's voice rumbling like thunder and see the wide smile that brightened his face and warmed his dark brown eyes. From that day on, the whole family had dreamed of owning the Fulton place. They made elaborate, happy plans. When they moved in, they'd trim the trees in the apple orchard, wallpaper the parlor, lay a new brick walk to the front porch.

Mandy's chest tightened, remembering. It had been three years since her father had boarded the train that spring day in 1943. She and her mother and Ira had stood there clinging to each other, watching him ride away from them, not knowing it was forever. When he'd been killed in Germany, their lives had been shattered in an instant, like glass smashed with a hammer, all splinters and pain, and impossible to put together again.

Mandy's gaze focused again on the bills in her hands. Their plans had been so exciting, so sure. Now the money was all she had left. Her father was gone and their dream was slipping away. But even though her mother seemed to have given up the idea of owning the Fulton place, Mandy couldn't let go. She was convinced that it was the only place where she could be close to her father. Every time she thought of it, her father seemed to come clear in her mind. For those few moments, he was as real and bright as the lamp's flame. Mandy closed her eyes and concentrated on the single, crystal thought spinning around and around in her head. Dreams don't just happen; you have to make them come true.

chapter ❧ two

*B*y the time Mandy came downstairs for breakfast, her mother had left for the store. Ira was at the table, working on a stack of pancakes. As she slid into her chair, Mandy leaned over and whispered to him, "Ira, will you braid my hair when you finish eating?"

She liked her hair braided and out of the way, but it was almost impossible for her to do it herself. Though Ira was maddeningly slow, he was neat, when she could talk him into doing it.

"Aw, Mandy, your hair's all right like that."

"What is it?" Aunt Bess asked, coming over to the table. Mandy glared at Ira and shook her head in a silent warning, even though she knew he wasn't one to keep still. His thoughts, secret or not, usually spilled out of his brain like water out of an overturned bucket.

"Mandy wants me to braid her hair. Boys aren't supposed to do that kind of stuff, are they, Aunt Bess?"

What in the world's got into him? Mandy fumed. He'd never balked at doing it before. Just wait, she resolved, until he wants me to do something for him!

"When there's work to be done, you just do it," Aunt Bess replied, frowning. Then as if to prove her words, she stepped over behind Mandy and began plaiting Mandy's hair into a single, thick braid. As she finished, Mandy handed her the rubber band to secure the end.

"Thanks," Mandy mumbled, angry at Ira and Aunt Bess both. She didn't want any favors from either of them.

After breakfast, Mandy and Ira set out for the store, taking their time on the sunny road. Along the stream by the lane, willows glowed with pale green buds. Sparrows and robins and newly arrived bluebirds were as excited as children at Christmas. They flitted from tree limb to fence post, broadcasting their own sweet announcement of spring. Despite the day's promise, Mandy saw only the bleak days and weeks ahead.

"I wish we were back in Garnet Creek," she said more to herself than to Ira. "In the Fulton house."

"We're never gonna live there now," Ira said in a matter-of-fact tone. His next words were not so positive. "Unless Dad comes home."

Mandy stopped and stared at her brother, her breath tight in her chest. "Ira, you should know by now, he's not coming home," she said, letting anger burn away the familiar pain.

"But he might. They could've made a mistake."

Mandy let out a noisy breath. "He's dead, Ira, and he's never coming home."

Ira stared at her a moment, then with head bent and hands in his pockets, he walked on.

Mandy ran to catch up. "I'm sorry, Ira, but it's the truth."

"Yeah," was all he said, but a moment later he looked over at her and smiled. That smile did more to brighten Mandy's day than the sun and the birds combined. After all, he was the only friend she had here.

A short walk down the paved county road brought them to the highway and the store. The store building, almost twice as long as it was wide, faced the paved road and the railroad beyond. A tall, flat-roofed canopy shaded the front steps and the benches on either side.

Ira led the way into the large room with its high ceiling and squeaky wooden floors. As Mandy's eyes adjusted to the gloom, she gazed around her. Shelves lined both long walls from floor to roof. They were filled with cans and boxes, all the usual goods found in any country store. Counters on either side marked off a central walkway. Boxes and crates cluttered the center aisle, along with buckets, kegs of nails, even a garden push plow.

Mandy noticed a young woman behind the counter. It was clear that she was going to have a baby soon. She must be Stella Fry, the clerk her mother had mentioned. As Mandy watched, Stella reached down into the silver-topped cooler and came up with a fat scoop of chocolate ice cream. She forced it into the cone she was holding, then handed it to a small girl peeping over the counter. As she took the girl's nickel, she looked over at Mandy and smiled.

Mandy nodded and went on until she came to the glass-enclosed candy counter. In one corner of the case above a box of candy bars, she saw an elaborate spiderweb, and among the hair-fine threads, the spider who had crafted it. Now she understood what her mother meant when she said there was lots to be done. The place must not have been cleaned in months.

Before Mandy could explore further, her mother came toward her, saying, "I've left you the job of scrubbing out the post office boxes, Mandy." She pointed to a scrub bucket already filled with water, then left to give Ira directions about what she wanted done in the basement.

The post office occupied a tiny room at the back of the store, a walled-in space with a low ceiling, a room within a room. Its front wall was a honeycomb of metal boxes, open inside the room, with small, locked doors on the outside that gave people access to their mail. A sliding window opened into the store; through it people could buy stamps and mail packages.

Mandy went into the post office and set to work. There were ninety-six mailboxes, but by the time she'd scrubbed twenty of them, she wished she hadn't counted. When she'd finally finished with the mailboxes, she used the tattered broom she found leaning in the corner to dust down the cobwebs and sweep the floor.

Wondering what to do with the scrub water, she looked through the sliding window for her mother. She was busy with a customer, so Mandy leaned on the window counter and waited. She could see every part of the store and everyone who came or departed. As she watched the activity, a boy about her own age entered the front door. Mud from his shoes left a dirty trail all the way down the center aisle. There was mud on his trousers too, and his shirt sleeves were rolled up to his elbows, as if he'd just finished some heavy chore.

As Mandy turned toward her mother again, she heard coins clattering along the wooden countertop and dropping on the floor. She saw her mother hurry out from behind the counter to gather up the scattered money. The muddy boy went to help, crawling across the floor on his hands and knees. After several moments, he rose and reached out a hand to Mandy's mother. "Here's four pennies."

Mandy's eyes widened. She'd watched the whole thing and was sure she'd seen him pick up a quarter. The boy slid his hands into his pockets and when he spoke, his words were loud enough for Mandy to hear. "I wonder if you have any work. I've done some jobs for Mr. Armstrong before."

"I'm sorry," Mandy's mother said. "I've got two children of my own and they'll be helping me. Sorry."

The boy nodded and turned toward the door, and Mandy hurried out into the store. Her mother wouldn't feel sorry for him when she found out he'd stolen some of her money.

"Oh, you must be mistaken, Mandy," her mother said.

"No, I'm not. I saw him pick up a quarter," Mandy said.

"What's wrong?" Stella asked, joining Mandy in front of the counter.

"Mama dropped some coins on the floor and a boy helped pick them up. But he didn't give all of them back."

"Are you talking about the boy who just left?" Stella asked.

"Yes," Mandy said. "He picked up a quarter, but all he gave Mama was pennies."

Stella nodded with a smile. "That's Dean Sanders. He lives on the farm next to your Aunt Bess." She straightened her faded apron, then added, "We have to watch him. He takes things."

Stella's comment convinced Mandy that the boy had kept some of the money. There was nothing to be done about this theft, but at least now they knew he couldn't be trusted.

There were so many things to do that it was late afternoon when Mandy's mother reminded her about the sheep. Mandy took her time walking back to the farm. She didn't stop at the house because she dreaded seeing Aunt Bess even more than she did the sheep.

Aunt Bess had said the sheep were let out in the early spring, not so much to graze as to walk the hills and get in condition for lambing. Mandy scanned the pasture for them, trying to imagine being close to them. They were probably dirty and smelly, like all the other farm animals she'd ever encountered. She wrinkled her nose at the thought.

With the sun warming her back, she began to climb. The land was brown with last year's weeds, but Mandy knew when spring came to the Ohio hills, it happened almost overnight. One day there was snow, the next day a tinge of green. She breathed in the clean air that already carried the hint of apple blossoms and violets and tender grass.

A bleating chorus sounded from the hillside and Mandy looked up and saw the flock heading her way, a few sleek yearlings and the round-bellied, pregnant ewes. They seemed to know she had come for them. The sheep moved toward her, rippling and flowing together like a school of fish in an unseen current. Aunt Bess had said that where one went, they all went. They must be awful dumb, Mandy thought, watching their endless shifting and maneuvering to stay together.

Aunt Bess had cautioned her to count the flock every day, to make sure none had been injured and left behind. Mandy counted fifty-two as they swarmed down the hillside. There should be fifty-three. She counted again but the tally was the same. She watched their approach, trying to swallow down the thick lump in her throat.

The sheep milled around her, bleating, gazing up at her with curious eyes. She lifted her hands high up on her chest, aching to run from them, holding her breath against the barnyard smell of manure and musty hay that hung in the air. A few bold animals came and sniffed her clothes, and one even nibbled at her pant leg. She finally gathered enough nerve to push it away. The wool felt greasy, despite its crusty layer of dirt.

By the time Mandy had counted again and still come up one short, the animals had lost interest in her and begun drifting toward the barn. She let out a long, easing breath, then started up the hill in search of the missing sheep.

She had not gone far when a wail, almost like a baby's cry, sounded a short distance above her.

Skirting around a clump of briars, she found a ewe lying on the ground with two small, white lambs beside her.

Mandy had never seen any newborn lambs up close. Soft and wet, with tight, wavy wool, they were surely only minutes old. Though they tried to stand, their thin, bony legs wouldn't hold them up. Seeing Mandy, the mother sheep struggled to her feet. There was a V-shaped notch about the size of Mandy's thumbnail along the upper edge of one ear and a tuft of wool standing upright on top of her head. She eyed Mandy for a moment, then bent and began licking one of the lambs.

Mandy watched, fascinated, until she realized that the sun had dropped behind the hill. It would be dark soon, and she had to get the family of sheep back to the barn. But how? The lambs were not yet able to walk. She stood there in the twilight, trying to decide what to do. Finally, though she cringed at the thought, Mandy knew there was only one solution. She would have to carry them. But she couldn't carry two lambs at the same time; each one was an armload. She'd just have to take one down, then come back for the other.

She edged closer, wondering what sheep did when they attacked. Did they kick or bite or maybe butt like a goat? With a wary eye on the mother sheep, Mandy bent down and picked up the nearest lamb. She cradled it against her stomach with its long legs dangling down to her knees. Strangely, it did not struggle at all, but lay motionless, black eyes blinking. Mandy could feel its fluttering heartbeat beneath her hand.

When the ewe made no move toward her, Mandy set off down the hill, bearing the load not much heavier than a bucket of water. A plaintive sound made her turn and look back. The ewe had started out after Mandy, but then had stopped, bewildered by the problem of her separated lambs. Mandy laid the lamb on the ground, then climbed back up the hill. With the other lamb secure in her arms, she made her way down in the fading light, the ewe following, giving an occasional bleat of protest.

Carrying one lamb for a distance, then doubling back for the other, Mandy was able to keep an eye on all three and still get them back to the barn before full dark.

Aunt Bess met her at the barn door. "Here, give me the lamb. I have a place for it over in the corner."

"There's another one," Mandy said.

"Well, go get it," Aunt Bess directed. "The ewe will follow you in."

The new family was soon settled in the pen Aunt Bess had made by leaning an old gate across one corner of the barn. Mandy smiled as she watched them. The lambs were able to stand now and began nosing their mother in search of milk.

"Where did you find them?" Aunt Bess asked, bringing the new mother a scoop of oats.

"Up on the hill, behind some briars," Mandy said. "Do they always have their lambs out in the pasture field?"

"No, I just didn't expect any this early." Aunt Bess faced Mandy, her eyes pale blue ice. "When they're ready to drop their lambs, I bring them in the barn."

Mandy made no response, sensing that Aunt Bess was mad at her, though she didn't know why.

"I've got Ned McGuire coming next week to shear them," Aunt Bess went on. "Maybe none of the other ewes will lamb before then."

"What happened to the ewe's ear?" Mandy asked.

"Oh, she ripped it on a barbed wire fence last summer."

Mandy ventured another question. "Do any of the sheep have names?"

"Names? Goodness sakes," Aunt Bess said. "I don't have time for such foolishness." And she went off to see about the rest of the flock.

Mandy wished she'd never asked any questions. They'd been there only a day, but already she knew how Aunt Bess felt about her. It doesn't matter, Mandy thought, because I don't like her either. She was cranky and seemed to find fault with every-thing. Even with the sheep. Instead of being pleased with the twin lambs, she complained about them coming early.

Mandy lingered by the sheep pen until Aunt Bess left for the house. Watching the lambs' awkward exploring, she felt a warmth steal over her. They were so small and weak, so helpless. A full-grown sheep might be frightening, but there was nothing to fear from a lamb. She reached out a hand to the nearest newborn. Its nose inched forward to touch her fingers, then it leaned back against its mother's side and closed its eyes. If such a frail, defenseless animal can get by, Mandy thought, then so can I, in spite of Aunt Bess.

A few moments later, Mandy stepped out into the starry night. The Milky Way was a smoky white splash across the black sky. Everything else might be strange here, Mandy thought, but the stars were as familiar and reliable as a robin in the spring.

chapter ✢ three

*T*he next morning on their way to the store, Mandy and Ira stopped at the barn to see the new lambs. They were awake, but remained safely hidden behind their mother. The mother sheep had more courage than her young. She came and laid her chin on the top board of the gate and gazed at Mandy. The ewe had lost her roundness and looked bony and lean.

Ira picked up a handful of hay and held it under her nose. "Come on, take it," he said. "It's good."

The ewe wiggled her ragged ear, but her coal black eyes remained fastened on Mandy, as if she remembered who had carried in her lambs.

The sheep's calm, curious gaze suddenly reminded Mandy of Mildred Gale back in Garnet Creek. Mildred, a spinster who lived in a little house beside the railroad track, seemed to accept whatever happened to her with trusting patience. She never complained. "The sun comes up sooner or later in everyone's sky," she'd remark about other people's misfortunes and her own as well. Mandy liked her spunk.

"If you had a name, I'll bet it'd be Mildred," she said. Still the ewe watched her and waited. "She wants some real food," Mandy said, and went to the feed bin and grabbed a handful of oats. Returning to the pen, she opened her fist and held out the grain in a flat hand, as she'd seen Aunt Bess do.

The ewe sniffed the end of her fingers, then daintily nibbled at the grain until she had gathered it all into her mouth. As Mandy wiped her wet palm on her dress, the ewe began chewing, gazing up with such solemn eyes that Mandy couldn't help laughing. "You're a pig, Mildred," she said.

"What's going on here?" came Aunt Bess's voice from the doorway. "I thought you two were on your way to the store."

"We are," Ira replied. "We just stopped by to see the lambs . . . and Mildred," he finished with a grin.

"Mildred?" Aunt Bess looked puzzled.

"Yeah, Mandy named the mother sheep Mildred."

Aunt Bess's unblinking gaze swung from Ira to Mandy. "You'd better get going. Your mother will be looking for you."

Mandy and Ira worked all morning with their mother, cleaning the store's windows and shelves and cupboards. They scrubbed the countertops with a brush and soapy water, and rearranged goods on the tall shelves. Mandy liked being behind the counter. It reminded her of the times she and Ira had played store with only a board across two sawhorses and some rusty washers for money. Now she could be a real clerk, once her mother showed her what to do.

"Mr. Armstrong will be surprised when he comes in tomorrow," Mandy's mother said. "He hasn't been able to do much cleaning lately."

"I thought he was going to have an operation," Mandy said.

"He is, the middle of next week."

"How soon will he be able to come back to work?" Mandy asked. When her mother gazed at her without answering, Mandy blushed. "I don't care," she blurted out. "The sooner he gets well, the sooner we can go back to Garnet Creek."

"We won't be going back to Garnet Creek until fall. That's already been decided." Her mother's blunt remark told Mandy the conversation was over.

They returned to the farm in late afternoon, and Mandy set off at once to get the sheep. The flock was nowhere in sight, and she wondered how far she'd have to go to find them. By the time she reached the top of the hill, she was breathing hard. She paused to catch her breath and look out over the greening land.

A stream wandered down the valley, an occasional

willow marking its course. At one point, the stream divided, flowing around either side of a grassy rise, then converging below it. From her vantage point, Mandy could see the small island's perfect teardrop shape. Sometime she'd walk up the valley and wade over to it. It'd be fun to be all alone on your own little island.

Mandy's gaze followed a rusty ribbon of road past scattered farmhouses and barns and slender, domed silos. Directly across the valley from Aunt Bess's house stood the weathered schoolhouse, topped by a square bell tower. Mandy couldn't remember hearing the bell on Friday, though she'd seen the children outside at recess, and heard their distant shouting. She didn't want to think about going to school tomorrow. Everyone there would be a stranger.

Mandy turned and looked across the top of the hill for the sheep. She didn't see any animals, but she saw their trail leading off through the grass. Following it over the crest of the hill, she almost tripped over a sheep hidden by a clump of last year's weeds. It looked up at her, but did not attempt to stand. Mandy stopped to listen. The other sheep must be nearby, though all she heard was the hilltop wind, and from far away, a cow lowing.

If she couldn't find the sheep, maybe they could find her. She lifted her head and gave a long, lingering call. "Whoooee." There was only silence. Just as she prepared to call again, she saw them. Rounded, gray shapes came into view over the curve of the hill, hurrying, as if to greet an old friend.

Suddenly surrounded, Mandy clamped her jaws tight and waited for them to finish their sniffing investigation. Finally they wandered away. When the solitary sheep made no move to go with them, Mandy went back and looked at it more closely. Maybe it was about to have a lamb. She soon dismissed that idea. The animal was too sleek and muscular; it had to be one of the yearlings. Maybe if she went with the rest of the flock, it would follow.

As she began to move away, she heard a noise behind her and spun around. Coming along the path was the boy she'd seen at the store, the boy Stella had called Dean Sanders. He looked from her to the sheep on the ground.

"Something wrong?" he asked, as if meeting on a pasture path was as natural as meeting on a road.

Mandy didn't know whether to admit she knew him or pretend he was a stranger. They *were* strangers! She'd only seen him once, and he'd never seen her at all. Still, she felt she knew him quite well. She knew he was a thief. But right now she had a more important problem.

"This sheep won't go with the others," she replied.

Dean knelt down and placed a hand under the sheep's chin. He ran his other hand along the top of its head, over its ears, and down one of its front legs. Then pushing the woolly head to one side, he rolled the animal over so that it rested on its back between his knees.

"Here's the problem." He pointed to the back leg. "I think it's broken." He cradled the leg in his hand and worked his fingers through the greasy wool. A brief shudder was the animal's only reaction.

"Yeah, we'll have to tie it up. Can you find a stick about this long," he held his hands about a foot apart, "and this big around." He made a small circle with his thumb and finger.

Mandy nodded and began searching among the weeds. When she returned with the stick, Dean was pulling off his outer shirt. He placed the stick along the sheep's leg and bound them together with the shirt.

"Now we need something to hold it. Do you have a belt . . . or a piece of string?" he asked Mandy.

"No," she replied, then remembered the thick rubber band on her braid. She pulled it off and handed it to him. He stretched it double between his fingers, then slipped it over the bandage.

"That'll hold it till we get back to the barn." He looked up at Mandy and said, "This is one of Bess Laney's sheep, isn't it?"

"Yes," Mandy said. She was lucky he'd come along, but how were they going to get the sheep back to the barn? Dean's abrupt move surprised her. He lifted the injured animal over his head, then let it down gently across his shoulders, its legs sticking out like tree branches in front of him. Clasping the sheep's three good legs against his chest, he stood up and motioned Mandy to lead the way.

Even as she accepted his help, Mandy was remembering what he'd done at the store. She felt guilty, knowing that about him, but that was silly, she told herself. He was the one who ought to feel guilty.

"I was working on the fence when I heard your call," he said.

"I didn't know where to look for the sheep, so I thought maybe they would come if I called," Mandy said.

"Next time you go after them, put a handful of grain in your pocket. When you find them, give them a few bites. Then they'll always come when you call."

Mandy turned and smiled back at him. "Thanks. I never thought of that."

"You related to Bess Laney?" he asked.

"Yes, she's my great-aunt. We just moved here last Friday . . . me and my mother and my brother, Ira." Mandy felt her face redden. Why was she giving him her life story?

"I guess you and your brother will go to our school then," he said.

"Yes, we'll start tomorrow," Mandy said.

Swinging down the hill, Mandy longed to fill the awkward silence, but she couldn't think of a thing to say.

"I'm going to have my own flock of sheep someday," Dean said. "That's why I've been working on the fences. It takes a real good fence to keep sheep in."

"You seem to know a lot about them," Mandy said.

"I've been helping your Aunt Bess for a couple of years. My name's Dean Sanders."

"I know," Mandy replied. "I saw you yesterday."

"You did? Where?"

"I was working in the back of the store." Dean looked puzzled. "My mother is running the store . . . until Mr. Armstrong gets well again." Feeling bolder, Mandy added, "You helped my mother pick up some money she dropped."

He looked over at her, his blue eyes as cloudless as the sky above him. "I went down there to ask about work, but I guess your mother won't need me. She's got you and your brother to help her." His smile was honest, untroubled.

Mandy had been watching for some sign of guilt, some glimmer of regret when she mentioned the money. But Dean's clear, open gaze was not that of a thief. She could have been mistaken about him picking up a quarter. Anyway, it was too late to worry about it. She already liked him.

As they neared the barn, Aunt Bess came to the open doorway. "Hello, Dean," she said. "A sick one?"

"No, I think her leg is broken."

"Well, bring her in and we'll see," Aunt Bess replied. She led the way to an empty stall and Dean lowered the sheep into the straw. Aunt Bess removed the rubber band and handed it to Mandy, then unwound the shirt. After feeling up and down the leg, she nodded her head.

"It's broken, but just a simple fracture. I'll set it and put a splint on it. Hold her still," she told Dean. From a peg on the wall she took down a thin, metal strip, curved just right to fit around a sheep's leg. There were two attached belts to hold it in place.

Mandy knew by the way Aunt Bess worked that she had set broken bones before. Her long fingers eased the bone into place and strapped the splint around it. When she was finished, Dean settled the sheep so that the injured leg rested comfortably on the straw. The animal had made no sound through-out the ordeal and now lay motionless, her black eyes blinking up at them.

Aunt Bess leaned down and stroked the sheep's nose with her knuckles, murmuring, "You're all right now." The softness in her voice surprised Mandy.

"I'd better get on home," Dean said, grabbing his shirt and rising to his feet.

"Thanks for helping Mandy with the sheep," Aunt Bess said.

Mandy wanted to thank him too, so she followed

him through the barn door. "I'm glad you came along . . ." she began, then blushed when she ran out of words.

Dean's blue eyes reflected the fading light as he turned to face her. "What's your last name?" His blunt question caught her by surprise, and her response was equally blunt.

"Gates," she said.

"With a little more practice, Mandy Gates, you'll make a good sheep woman, like your Aunt Bess."

Mandy almost responded that she did not intend—in fact, had no desire—to be a sheep woman.

"By the way," Dean continued, "sheep are a lot more afraid of you than you are of them. All they want is something to eat and a place to get in out of the rain . . . just like the rest of us." He grinned at her.

Mandy looked away. Somehow he'd guessed that she was afraid of the sheep. It made her feel strange, knowing he could see inside her mind. Did he also know the thoughts that had entered her mind when she first saw him on the hill?

Out of the gloom came one last remark. "See you at school tomorrow."

Mandy went back to help Aunt Bess. The sheep were crowded around the troughs waiting for their evening ration of grain.

"Dean helps me with the sheep sometimes," Aunt

Bess said, scooping oats into a bucket. After a few moments, she went on. "He can fix just about anything mechanical. It's kind of a shame . . ." She stopped, as if she'd started something she didn't know how to finish.

"What's a shame?" Mandy prompted.

"Oh, his family. His mother is more interested in going places than in keeping a home. When Dean works for me, I usually invite him to stay and eat. Sometimes he acts as though he hasn't had a bite in days."

"What about his father?" Mandy asked, trying to construct a mental picture of Dean's family and his home.

"He's sick a lot, mainly from the drinking, but when he's well enough, he works on Brantley's dairy farm. Dean's lucky though. He's got a lot more horse sense than both of his parents put together."

"He told me he plans to get some sheep," Mandy said.

"Yes," Aunt Bess replied. "I promised him one of my pregnant ewes this spring . . . whenever he gets the money together. Where he'll get thirty dollars, I wouldn't know."

Mandy recalled the episode at the store, the money she thought he'd stolen. Maybe Aunt Bess knew him well enough to clear up her doubts.

"Stella says he takes things," she said.

"I've heard the gossip," Aunt Bess said with just a hint of disapproval in her voice, as if reprimanding Mandy for passing on such rumors. "But he's never taken anything from me. I accept people the way they are, good or bad, until they prove differently." Her cold, calculating stare seemed to say that she had not yet decided in which category to place Mandy.

Back in her room later, Mandy's thoughts of Dean and the sheep and Aunt Bess faded before the worry of school the next day. She laid out her favorite dress and a matching ribbon for her braid. On the front of the new tablet she'd brought from the store, she wrote her name in neat, bold script. For a moment it felt like the beginning of a new school year, but they were actually closer to the end than the beginning. How she dreaded facing all those strangers, and the long, lonesome days of learning new ways and new people. Then she remembered Dean. At least one person at school wasn't a stranger.

chapter ❧ four

A cold drizzle fell as Mandy and Ira walked with their mother toward the school, and by the time they arrived, their coats were wet and heavy. A school bus pulled off the road behind them and when the door opened, children poured out like bees from a hive. Aunt Bess had told Mandy and Ira that they weren't eligible to ride the bus because her farm was too close to the school. It wasn't more than half a mile and Mandy didn't mind walking. Except on a rainy day. A person could get pretty wet in half a mile.

A few students stood under the roof covering the school steps and stared at Mandy and Ira, but none of them gave a sign of a greeting. Mandy knew her face was red, and felt it redden even more as anger burned away her embarrassment. If they still lived in Garnet Creek, she wouldn't be on exhibit this way, like a cow at the County Fair.

Just as they mounted the steps, a short, gray-haired woman stepped outside and began ringing a rusty cowbell. She stopped when she saw the three of them. Her smile, revealing a gold front tooth, was a sunbeam on this dismal day. "Hello, I'm Mrs. Nichols. I teach the lower grades." Her glance skipped from Mandy to Ira. "Would you be in the fourth?" she asked him.

Ira nodded and grinned. Mandy was glad for the woman's smile, even for that gold tooth. Maybe her teacher would be as nice as Mrs. Nichols seemed to be.

"I've got a desk I've been saving for my next new pupil. You don't mind if it's in the back of the room, do you?"

Ira shook his head and grinned again. He looked over at Mandy and lifted his eyebrows as if to say, "How's that for luck?"

With Ira settled in, Mandy and her mother climbed the dark steps to the upstairs classroom. Windows on the side walls and one at the back illuminated the big room, despite the cloudy day. In a sweeping glance, Mandy took in the old piano, the rows of wooden desks, the potbellied stove, the teacher's desk. Then her breath caught in her throat. She'd never even considered that her teacher might be a man.

Half hidden behind an open newspaper, he appeared unperturbed by the racket of the school day beginning. When he looked up and saw Mandy and her mother, he rose to his feet. He was tall with graying hair, and brown eyes that glimmered with welcome. Mandy's mother was the first to speak.

"I'm Mrs. Gates and this is my daughter, Mandy. She's in the seventh grade."

"I'm Bob Mills. Nice to meet you." His glance shifted over to Mandy, and Mandy felt her face redden again.

While her mother talked with him, Mandy looked around the room. She thought she might see Dean, but he must not have arrived yet. Her glance shied away from the curious stares, and she tried to ignore several girls giggling and whispering behind their hands.

"I'll be leaving now, Mandy," her mother said. With a sinking feeling in her stomach, Mandy watched her go. She wished she could go too, all the way back to Garnet Creek.

"You may hang your coat in the cloakroom," Mr. Mills said, pointing to a door in the front corner. "Then we'll find you a desk and some books."

Mandy slipped into the small room. Coats hung from hooks on the walls, three and four deep. Opposite the door, a waist-high window looked out on the school yard and the road. Mandy could see Aunt Bess's house and barn across the valley. She thought of Mildred and the lambs, and wondered how the injured sheep was doing.

The cloakroom door swung open and a girl

entered wearing a coat several sizes too big for her. She gave Mandy a shy smile. "What grade are you in?" she asked.

"Seventh," Mandy replied, finally finding a hook.

"So am I. That makes two girls in seventh grade now, and three boys."

Dreading to go into the classroom again, Mandy paused and said, "My name is Mandy Gates."

"I'm June Calley. Does Mandy stand for Amanda?"

"Yes, but nobody calls me that," Mandy told her.

When June went out the door, Mandy followed and waited by the door until Mr. Mills looked up. He motioned her over, then pointed to a desk halfway down a row.

"You may have that middle desk in the seventh-grade row," he said. "I'll get your books in a few minutes." He glanced at his watch, then picked up a pencil and began tapping on a green, heart-shaped jar sitting on his desk. It rang like a bell. "It's nine o'clock," he announced.

Students scrambled for their seats, then the room grew so quiet that Mandy could hear the thud of her own heart. Everyone must be afraid of Mr. Mills, she concluded. When he turned his back on the classroom, it seemed to be a signal for the students to stand up. They faced the flag that hung on the front wall over the blackboard and began reciting the Pledge of Allegiance. Rising, Mandy joined in, her voice just above a whisper.

Once everyone was seated again, Mr. Mills went to the blackboard and began writing. The room came alive with the rustle of papers and the dull clatter of pencils on desktops.

June occupied the front desk of Mandy's row and between them was a broad-shouldered boy in a red flannel shirt. In the row next to the windows, Mandy counted six big boys, eighth graders, she guessed. They fidgeted and squirmed, arms and legs in endless motion, as restless as tied rabbit dogs.

Mr. Mills brought Mandy an arithmetic book and gestured to the assignment he had written on the blackboard. She went to work on the page of division problems. They were easy and for a time helped her forget the strangeness of the place and her aching loneliness.

A little later, Mr. Mills brought her a stack of books: history, geography, science, a bright green reader. He bent over her desk and leafed through the history book until he found the page he wanted. "This is the chapter we'll be discussing today, so you can go ahead and start reading."

He wandered away and had just reached the far side of the room when footsteps sounded on the stairs. Heads lifted, waiting, and a moment later Dean stepped through the door. "Please continue your work," came Mr. Mills's clipped command to the classroom.

Mandy watched Dean slip out of his coat and saunter into the cloakroom. When he reappeared moments later, Mr. Mills motioned him over. Mandy couldn't hear what was said, but she saw Dean shrug his shoulders, then head for the back of the room. He came down the aisle, sticking his finger in the inkhole of each desk he passed. When he got to Mandy, he paused long enough to straighten the pile of books on top of her desk, then grinned at her and continued on.

Mandy blushed and wondered if the teacher had noticed. Her question was answered when Mr. Mills's voice sliced across the room. "Dean, the arithmetic assignment is on the board. I suggest you get started."

"I can't," came the easy reply. "I don't have any paper."

Mr. Mills frowned, his eyes never leaving Dean. "Mr. Armstrong sells tablets at his store."

"Mr. Armstrong's not selling anything anymore. He's sick," Dean informed him.

Mr. Mills's carefully controlled words were meant to end the matter. "David, will you give Dean a sheet of paper so he can do his work. I'd hate to see him have to spend a third year in the seventh grade."

Mandy heard the boy just behind her tear a sheet of paper out of his tablet and pass it back. Dean's polite response could he heard all over the room. "Thank you. Do you have an extra pencil?"

Mandy lowered her head, hiding her smile. At least one person in the room was not afraid of Mr. Mills.

Later in the morning when Mr. Mills sounded recess on his glass bell, there was a wild dash for the cloakroom. Mandy waited until it cleared out, then got her coat and went outside to find Ira. He'd already made friends with a sandy-haired boy he called Tappy, and they went off to play catch with Tappy's ball.

The rain had stopped, though dark clouds still hovered low over the valley. Mandy leaned on the corner of the schoolhouse and watched the activity around her. She saw June Calley leave a group of girls by the well and come toward her. June's round face and wide eyes made Mandy think of an owl, and she couldn't help but smile. June smiled back.

"Is that your brother?" she asked, pointing to Ira running after the ball.

"Yes. His name is Ira," Mandy replied.

"I guess you don't know anybody here yet."

"I know Dean Sanders," Mandy said. "He helped me yesterday with one of my aunt's sheep."

June giggled. "Everyone knows Dean."

As Mandy was pondering what that giggle could mean, Mrs. Nichols came to the door ringing her cowbell. Mandy let the stampeding students pass her by and took her time climbing the stairs.

When she came out of the cloakroom, she saw

Dean in the back, elbows on the desk, his chin resting in his cupped hands. Mr. Mills must have made him stay in at recess for being tardy. Dean's roving eyes stopped on Mandy and he smiled. She nodded and went on to her seat. From what the teacher had said earlier, this was Dean's second year in the seventh grade. No wonder! He came late and didn't even bring pencils or paper to do his work. As she slipped into her seat, she saw him turn sideways in his seat and gaze out the window. She had the feeling he would much rather have been up on the hill mending fences.

In the afternoon, following a discussion of Abraham Lincoln, Mr. Mills gave the seventh grade the rest of the week's history assignments. In addition to reading two chapters from the textbook, they must memorize the Gettysburg Address and be able to recite it on Friday. It was not printed in their texts, but Mr. Mills had a copy. He read it aloud to them, then handed it to June, indicating she should copy it and pass it back.

After Mandy copied the speech and handed it to the boy behind her, she realized school would be dismissed before it got to Dean. He probably didn't have any paper anyway. She took out her tablet and recopied the speech, then folded it and wrote Dean's name on the outside. Reaching over her shoulder, she laid it on the desk behind her so that Dave could read the name and hand it back to

Dean. Now we're even, Mandy thought. He helped me with the sheep; I helped him with his history lesson. A moment later, Mr. Mills tapped his bell and the room erupted into noisy confusion. As Mandy entered the cloakroom, Dean came in behind her, holding the folded copy of the speech.

"Thanks for this," he said, "but I don't do much homework. I always find more interesting things to do." His eyes steadied on hers and the corners of his mouth curved upward, as if he found everything, including Mandy, amusing. He's laughing at me, Mandy thought, for wasting my time making him a copy. He probably knew from the moment Mr. Mills assigned the speech that he wasn't going to memorize it. Mandy shrugged and went out the door. If Dean wanted to flunk seventh grade again, it was none of her business.

chapter ❧ five

*M*andy peeped in the downstairs classroom, but the only persons there were Mrs. Nichols and a girl erasing the blackboard. Ira was probably waiting for her outside. As soon as she stepped through the door, she could hear the noisy crowd. What she saw set her heart to hammering. Out on the playground, Ira stood inside a jostling circle of children, one of the eighth-grade boys towering over him.

"What's going on?" It was June beside her.

"My brother . . ."

"Yeah, and Curtis Jones," June finished.

Mandy took off at a run and pushed her way through to the inner circle just as Curtis knocked a book out of Ira's hand.

"Ira! What kind of name is that for a boy?" he asked. Fire blazed in her brother's eyes as Mandy stepped over beside him. She picked up his book and put it on top of her own.

"Well, here's the big sister," Curtis said, grinning down at Mandy and grabbing for her braid.

With a toss of her head, Mandy evaded his hand. Before she could speak, Ira stepped forward, an angry, bristling bulldog. "You leave my sister alone."

Mandy seized Ira's arm to pull him back, but he jerked away from her. There was no way to stop Curtis, so she had to stop Ira. "The first day of school and you're already in trouble," she scolded him. "What'll Mama say?"

"Well, he's got Tappy's ball and he won't give it back."

Mandy's darting glance located Tappy at the edge of the crowd, white-faced, chewing on his bottom lip. He was even smaller than Ira.

"Both of you together couldn't stand up to him," Mandy said, waving a hand at Curtis.

As she and Ira stood glaring at each other, June elbowed her way in front of them. Her low-pitched voice cut through the crowd noise, patient, commonplace. "Curtis, give Tappy his ball so we can all go home."

Curtis's eyes slid over to her, then back to Mandy. He tossed the ball a foot or so into the air and without looking at it, caught it in one hand. While everyone watched, he continued his one-handed pitch and catch, enjoying his season of fame. But then as the ball went skyward once more, there was a sudden blur of motion between Mandy and Curtis, and a rumbling noise from the onlookers.

Dean had jumped forward and snatched the ball

in midair, then in a lightning-swift move, tossed it to Tappy. At the same moment that Tappy caught the ball, he spun around and disappeared into the crowd. Not knowing where the ball was, Curtis jumped at Dean and wrestled him to the ground. Dean squirmed away and sprang to his feet, his empty hands spread out before him. "I don't have it," he said.

Mandy didn't wait for any more trouble. "Let's get out of here," she said, pushing Ira ahead of her. This time he didn't resist. As they hurried out into the road, June ran up alongside. She and Mandy exchanged smiles that turned into giggles.

"What's so funny?" Ira demanded. When they didn't answer him, he went on. "I wasn't scared of him."

"Well, you should've been," Mandy said. "He could squash you like a ripe tomato."

Ira turned to June. "You're not scared of him."

June's smile was serene. "He knows better than to pick on me. I have an older brother."

The three of them paused and looked back toward the school. They could see Curtis standing alone, waving his arms at someone going the other direction on the road. It was Dean, strolling along with his hands in his pockets, unbothered, unhurried. Even when Curtis began throwing stones at him, Dean did not alter his leisurely pace.

"You live over this direction?" Mandy asked June.

"Up that way," June said, pointing ahead to where the road divided and the right fork climbed around a tree-covered hill. "About a mile. Across the road from the sawmill."

"We're living with Aunt Bess," Mandy said, waving a hand at the farmhouse in the distance.

"I know Mrs. Laney. She's nice," June said.

Mandy didn't know whether to agree or disagree, so she remained silent. At the fork in the road, June stopped.

"See you tomorrow," she said, then added with a smile. "And don't forget the Gettysburg Address."

Mandy smiled back, feeling a sudden twinge of sadness. June's smile reminded her of Sally, her best friend back in Garnet Creek. It seemed like they'd been gone from there for months, but it had been only four days. She wouldn't see Sally again until fall, unless they went back to visit. Would she and Sally still be best friends after all that time? Mandy wondered. It just wasn't fair, having to leave friends and go to live with strangers.

Walking up Aunt Bess's lane, Ira turned to Mandy. "What's wrong with my name?"

"There's nothing wrong with it," Mandy growled. "It was Dad's name, wasn't it?"

"Yeah," Ira said, dropping his head and kicking at a piece of gravel. "Mandy . . ." He looked up at her with probing eyes that hoped to read in her face the right answer to his question. "Do you think Dad

might . . . I mean, could he still be alive somewhere?"

Mandy let out her breath to loosen the tightness
in her chest. She knew only one answer to give him.
It was cruel and final. "No."

The icy word hung there between them until
finally Ira blurted out, "You don't know everything,"
and he took off running, disappearing into the
house long before Mandy reached the yard.

Mandy wished he could accept the truth, but sometimes she envied him that impossible, marvelous
hope that their father still lived. Their father's
death was a certainty. Mandy knew that, because the
knowledge of it lay in a dark, cold corner of her
mind, ice that never melted.

The day he'd gone away, the last day she'd seen
him alive, he'd promised to return. "Don't worry,"
he'd said to her. "I'll be back." But it was a lie.

A pain shuddered through Mandy, stirring up a
white-hot anger. I'm sorry, Dad, she spoke in her
mind to the shadowy face she couldn't quite recall,
but you shouldn't have promised. I trusted you and
you lied.

It was the first lie he'd ever told her. And the last,
Mandy thought, grinding her teeth together. She
pushed away the memory of her father with the
same coldhearted deliberation she'd used to tell Ira
their father was dead. She wouldn't think about
him; it hurt too much.

Mandy heard Aunt Bess in the kitchen, but went straight on to her room. She didn't feel like facing Aunt Bess's silent criticism either. After changing into her overalls, she stepped over to the window and looked for the sheep. There were several grazing along the top of the hill, so she knew the rest would be somewhere nearby.

Recalling Dean's advice about taking some grain along when she went after the sheep, Mandy filled one pocket with oats, then set out across the pasture. She was close to the animals before they saw her, but she called anyway. "Whoooee . . ." The ewe closest to her, round and heavy with unborn young, came toward her at an awkward trot.

"You'd better not bite," Mandy muttered as the sheep approached her. Pulling some oats from her pocket, she held them out in her flattened hand. The ewe did not hesitate, but came at once and gobbled up every kernel. Soon the others crowded around her. As she fed them the rest of the oats, she counted. They were all there. Including the four in the barn, Aunt Bess's flock now numbered fifty-five. And from the looks of the big-bellied ewes, there would soon be plenty more.

Later, when Mandy entered the kitchen door, Aunt Bess looked up from the potato she was peeling. "Mandy, I've laid out clean sheets on the beds. I want you to go up and change them—you'll have time before supper. I thought Ira could help you but he's gone to the store."

Mandy nodded and headed for the stairs. She didn't mind making beds, but she resented Aunt Bess's bossy tone of voice, without even a hint of appreciation in it. Aunt Bess never asked; she just gave orders.

Mandy made her bed first, then her mother's, deciding to leave Ira's until last. When he came home, he could help her with it, or better yet, make it himself.

Mandy had never been in Aunt Bess's bedroom, though she'd looked in sometimes when passing down the hall. The last bit of daylight filtering through the blinds gave the room a soft, golden glow. The bed had a wooden headboard and carved posts, taller than Mandy, rising at the corners.

Mandy finished making the bed and had started for the door when she noticed a shiny box on top of the chest of drawers. It gleamed like silver. Moving closer, she could see tiny flowers and leaves etched along the sides. She picked it up to examine it more closely. The raised figures of a man and woman decorated the top. Dressed in old-fashioned clothes, they stood close together, heads leaning toward each other, as though sharing some happy secret. Mandy rubbed her fingers across the sparkling design.

As she started to lift the lid, she heard a noise and turned to see Aunt Bess in the doorway. The dark anger in her aunt's face made Mandy feel as though she had committed a crime. Before she could say anything, Aunt Bess came and took the silver box out of her hands.

"You were to come in here and make my bed. That's all," she said. In the tense quiet, she placed the box back on top of the chest.

"I was just looking . . ." Mandy began.

Aunt Bess interrupted. "I saw what you were doing. Just because you live here doesn't give you the right to go through my personal things."

"I'm sorry . . . I didn't mean . . ."

"You're finished in here, so just go," Aunt Bess said.

Mandy put her hands out in front of her, wanting to explain, but Aunt Bess's cold, hard eyes defeated her. She left the room, blinking back tears.

Dashing down the stairs, she ran out the door and across the yard, slowing only when she reached the barn. Leaning her forehead against the rough boards, she shivered in the cool night air. How could Aunt Bess be so unjust? She hadn't been snooping. She'd simply looked at the chest sitting out in plain sight. Wouldn't she be surprised, Mandy thought, if she knew that I'm not the least bit interested in her or her belongings.

She clamped her chattering teeth together and

folded her arms against the chill. Maybe it was warmer inside the barn. Unfastening the door, she stepped inside. The barn's pungent odor burned her nose, like wood smoke from a campfire. She paused to listen for the sheep. Though her eyes could not penetrate the darkness, she could hear their breathing and champing and quiet stirrings.

She felt her way over to the lambs' pen. There was the rustle of straw, then something soft nuzzled her hand. Forgetting her fear, she stroked the ewe's nose and her fuzzy, notched ear. What was it Dean had said? All sheep wanted was something to eat and a place to get in out of the rain. But maybe they needed more than that, Mandy thought. Maybe they were like people and needed someone close to them, someone who cared about them.

Mandy stood there in the darkness, longing for someone to talk to, someone to listen. This place, Aunt Bess, the school, everything was even worse than she had imagined it would be. She felt like a sheep must feel when it was lost from the flock and didn't know how to get back to the barn. The next six months stretched ahead of her like a long, dark tunnel.

The ewe gave a mournful bleat. "Do you need a friend, Mildred?" Mandy murmured. She smiled then, thinking how ridiculous it was to be standing out here in pitch blackness, talking to a dumb animal. Deep down, she knew she was just trying to postpone going back to the house. But she'd have to face Aunt Bess sooner or later. I don't have to like her, she thought; I just have to get along with her. For as long as they lived here anyway. Once they were back in Garnet Creek, Aunt Bess could be forgotten, along with everyone else in this place. But for now, she'd have to apologize, even though she hadn't done anything wrong.

The animal warmth in the barn gradually stilled Mandy's shivering and though she couldn't see the sheep, their presence there in the darkness was real and comforting. Brushing her fingers over the ewe's damp nose one last time, she said, "Goodnight, Mildred," then turned toward the door. Crossing the yard, Mandy steeled herself to face Aunt Bess. She'd say she was sorry, even if it was a lie. Just as she reached for the doorknob, the door swung inward. Aunt Bess stood there frowning, her body stiff and straight. She must have been watching for Mandy.

"I want to apologize to you, Mandy," she said, her voice determined and low. "I said things I shouldn't have said."

"I came back to apologize to you," Mandy replied, finding it easier to say than she'd anticipated. Maybe it was because Aunt Bess appeared so uncomfortable.

Aunt Bess lowered her head and ran her hands down the front of her apron. Then she looked at Mandy again. "I was worried about you out in the cold without a coat."

Why would she worry about me, Mandy mused, when she doesn't even like me? She dropped her eyes to hide the thought. "I went into the barn. It was warm in there."

"Yes. The sheep keep the barn comfortable, even in the coldest weather."

Mandy edged toward the stairs, hoping to escape to her room, but Aunt Bess followed along behind her.

"How's Mildred?" she asked.

Was Aunt Bess actually calling a sheep by name? Mandy turned her face away to hide her smile. "Oh, she's just fine. Well, I've got homework to do . . ." she spoke over her shoulder.

"Yes, all right. I'll call you when it's time to set the table for supper."

Mandy climbed the stairs, puzzling over the woman she knew as Aunt Bess, but a person who still seemed more stranger than kin. Was it possible to live with other people and yet remain strangers? Mandy wondered. So far, Aunt Bess had done just that. She'd given them a place to live and plenty of food to eat. She provided for them in the same way she provided for her sheep, generously, but without letting her feelings be involved. But we're not sheep, Mandy thought. She had to be fair, though. After living alone all these years, Aunt Bess probably needed time to get used to having people around. Besides, when she'd accepted them into her home, maybe she hadn't considered she'd have to accept them into her life too.

chapter ❦ six

*L*ater, as Mandy was setting the table, her mother and Ira came in the back door. They shed their coats, then went to the sink to wash their hands. Mandy noticed how slowly her mother moved, how heavily she sank into the chair at the table. Mr. Armstrong was lucky to find someone like her, Mandy thought, someone who would work hard in the store as if it was her own. Mandy's mind raced across time to the day when they would leave this place. It would be a day to celebrate. She heard her name and looked up.

"Why didn't you stop it, Mandy?" her mother was saying.

"Stop what?"

"Ira told me what happened at school."

"I tried to stop them, Mama, but you know how he is." Her eyes slid over to Ira. He wrinkled his nose at her and grinned.

"Mandy, you're older and, hopefully, a little wiser."

"That Curtis Jones is a bully," Mandy declared, sliding into her chair.

"Well, all I know is, the two of you got into a scrape your first day in a new school."

Though Mandy could feel her mother's eyes on her, she didn't look up. "If we were back in . . ." she murmured into her plate.

"Mandy . . ." her mother began, then paused to fidget with her knife and fork. Her voice quivered with anger when she went on. "We'll be here until the last of August, Mandy. If you accept that, things will be easier for all of us."

Mandy stared hard at her mother, then met Aunt Bess's questioning gaze only a moment before looking back at her plate. She hated this place. Parrish Grove wasn't even a town, just a lot of dusty roads and helter-skelter houses and unpainted barns. Nobody would live here unless they had to, she silently concluded.

The next morning Mandy padded down the stairs in her pajamas, hoping to catch her mother before she left for the store. She'd tried doing her braid herself, but she just couldn't get it right. There were always straggling wisps of hair that she couldn't seem to capture. She was still angry with her mother, but she'd rather ask her mother to do it than Aunt Bess.

As she neared the bottom of the stairs, she heard Aunt Bess and her mother talking. She stopped because they were talking about her.

"She never mentions her father," Aunt Bess was saying. "And neither do you, Vera."

"What's the use, Aunt Bess. That part of our life is over."

"But you can't just act as if he'd never lived."

"It's easier to fill my mind with other things. It hurts so much to remember."

"Don't you think Mandy is hurting too?" Aunt Bess asked. "Don't you think she's missing him?"

"Please, Aunt Bess, don't make things any harder than they already are."

Unable to listen to any more, Mandy crept back up the steps and tiptoed down the hall to her room. She set to work on her hair, not caring how it turned out. Why didn't Aunt Bess mind her own business! They didn't need her to tell them what to talk about, what to remember. She was always trying to boss people, as if she knew better than anyone else what ought to be done. She doesn't need to feel sorry for me, either, Mandy thought, pulling her hair until it hurt.

It was late when Mandy descended the stairs, dressed for school, her hair in a loose, untidy braid. She grabbed a sliver of bacon and slipped on her coat. She was out the door so quickly that Ira had to run to catch her.

"What's your hurry?" he demanded. When she didn't answer, he said, "You know Curtis will be there."

"Yes, and you keep away from him," Mandy said. "If he takes Tappy's ball again, just stay out of it."

"I can't. Tappy's my friend."

"You've only known him one day," Mandy said. Ira sure was dumb if he thought friends were made in a day.

"He's my friend," Ira repeated.

Just then, Mandy looked up the road and saw June waiting for them at the crossroads. Her over-sized coat hung well below her knees, making her look, from a distance, like a little old woman.

Mandy felt a twinge of homesickness, longing for her friend, Sally. They'd grown up together and had always been best friends. No one else could take Sally's place. It's not even worth the trouble of trying to make friends here, Mandy reasoned, since we're only going to be in Parrish Grove until fall. Besides, it took years to make a best friend.

As they approached, June's face lit up with a smile. June might not be a real friend, Mandy thought, but seeing that smile did a lot to lift her sagging spirits.

"We'd better hurry," June said to them. "I think it's almost nine."

"Back in Garnet Creek they rang the bell at ten to nine," Mandy said, "and you could hear it all over town. Then we knew we had ten minutes to get to school."

"They used to ring a bell here too, but not any-more."

"Why not?" Ira asked.

"The rope broke," June replied, waving a hand at the bell tower. "The bell's still up there, but now Mrs. Nichols has her cowbell and Mr. Mills has his jar. I guess we don't need a bell."

"It'd be nice though," Mandy said, "and nobody would have an excuse for being late." It didn't make any sense to have a bell and not ring it. "We could get a rope and have one of the boys fix it," she suggested.

"I don't know what Mr. Mills would think," June said.

Mandy grinned at her. "Maybe if we told him it'd help Dean get to school on time, he'd be in favor of it."

After seeing Ira safely inside, Mandy and June ran up the stairs and hurried into the cloakroom. When they stepped out into the classroom moments later, June stopped so abruptly that Mandy bumped into her.

"I can't believe it!" June said, staring toward the back of the room, her owl eyes wide with surprise.

"What?" Mandy asked.

"Dean's already here," she said. "He hasn't been on time for weeks," she added.

Mandy leaned around to look. Dean was busy poking at the fire in the potbellied stove. His shirt was ragged at the elbows, but his hair had been wet down and combed into a wave over his forehead. Mandy wondered why he even bothered to come to school when he hardly ever did any school work.

Later, as she was digging in her desk for her arithmetic book, a shadow fell across her. She looked up into Dean's smiling face.

"I wonder if I could borrow a sheet of paper," he said. "I haven't got to the store yet."

Mandy nodded and bent over to find her tablet. "I'm glad you got Tappy's ball back yesterday." She tore out a sheet and handed it to him. "What happened after we left?"

"Nothing," he said. "Curtis is mostly talk."

"He's a bully," Mandy declared.

"Oh, he's all right . . . most of the time. Thanks for the paper," he said and turned away.

Puzzled by his kind remark about Curtis, Mandy watched Dean stroll down the aisle. He curled the sheet of paper into a slender tube, then stopped and held it to his eye like a spyglass, peering at something out the window. As he stood there, Mandy saw him reach down and pick up a pencil from the desktop. Then he went on to his seat. She glanced around the room, wondering who else had observed his casual theft. Apparently, he was going to get away with it . . . again.

She faced front, convinced once again that he'd kept some of the money her mother had dropped. Stella was right; he did have to be watched. It seemed strange, though, that he would borrow paper and steal a pencil.

Several times during the morning, Mandy cast a

sideways glance at Curtis, and not once did she see him looking in her direction. At recess he played ball with the other eighth graders. It was as if she and Ira didn't exist. Mandy was glad to be ignored, and she stayed as far from Curtis as she could get.

During seventh-grade history, Mr. Mills reminded them of their assignment to memorize the Gettysburg Address. "It's due on Friday," he said. He looked to the back of the room and said, "You have a question, Dean?"

"If someone learns it, can they say it before Friday?"

"Yes, we'll take time for the recitations whenever anyone is ready."

"I'm ready," Dean said.

There were soft sounds of surprise, even from the other side of the room. Mandy glanced around at Dean. He was leaning back with his elbows resting on the top of his seat, his eyes fastened on Mr. Mills.

"Very well, Dean. You may recite it now. There by your desk will be fine."

As Dean rose to his feet, Mandy turned her back on him and pulled out her copy of the speech. How could he have learned it so soon? She saw Mr. Mills lean back in his chair and fold his arms, a calm, closed expression on his face. Mandy could tell he was skeptical too.

His voice confident and easy, Dean recited the speech without one mistake. There was a long moment of silence, then Mr. Mills said, "Thank you, Dean."

Mandy let out a slow, quiet breath. She'd thought all along he was capable of doing his homework. If he'd learned that whole speech in one night, then he shouldn't have any trouble with his other work. She couldn't help wondering if her copying the speech for him had anything to do with his memorizing it.

The boy in front of Mandy raised his hand and when Mr. Mills nodded to him, he asked, "Where is Gettysburg?"

"If you look in your text, there is a map of the United States in the front," Mr. Mills said.

"Gettysburg's not on there," Dean spoke from the back. "I already looked."

"Well, it's in Pennsylvania. That's on your map," Mr. Mills responded. A hand went up in the eighth-grade row. "What is it, Curtis?"

"I was just wondering why we don't have one of them big maps that hang on the wall," he said. "I went to school with my cousin over in Pearlsburg, and they had a big, colored map of the whole United States." There was a rumble of approval from the other students.

Mr. Mills came around his desk. "There seems to be an unusual interest in geography today," he said, loud enough to include everyone in the room. Heads came up and all eyes fixed on him.

After a moment, he spoke to Curtis's question. "The money I was given for supplies this year has all been spent."

"We could earn some money . . . maybe," Curtis said.

Mr. Mills gazed at Curtis a long, unsettling time, then turned and opened one of his desk drawers. He pulled out a catalogue and began to leaf through it, then stopped and read down the page. When he looked up, everyone in the room seemed to lean forward a little in their seats.

"A wall map costs over a hundred dollars." The teacher paused to let the hushed noises subside.

"We could never get that much money," the boy in front of Mandy mumbled.

"Yes, we can," Curtis spoke up. "If each of us only made a dollar, we'd have almost half of it."

Mr. Mills silenced them all with a look. He came and stood just in front of June's desk, and everyone held their breath and waited for his next words.

"Are you willing to buckle down and work for it?" he asked.

There was a deafening burst of clapping, shouting, and whistling that made Mr. Mills smile even as he raised his hands for order. Once it was quiet again, he gazed around the room, inspecting every person there to make sure of their commitment.

"Between now and next Monday, I want everyone to be thinking of ways for us to make money . . .

some kind of fund-raiser, an activity where people will pay to participate."

There was a rising murmur of excitement, and Mr. Mills's smile only added to it. He reached for the green, heart-shaped jar on his desk and held it up so that everyone could see it.

"This will be our bank. If you want to donate some money, you may deposit it in here." He reached in his pocket and pulled out several coins and dropped them into the green jar. "This is the beginning of our map fund."

After school was over, Mandy and June headed for the cloakroom. Curtis came out the door, then turned and held it open for them, bowing as they passed. Mandy refused even to acknowledge his presence. By the time they had found their coats, Curtis had disappeared.

As she and June went down the stairs, Mandy said, "I hope my brother hasn't gotten into trouble again."

"Curtis didn't seem to be looking for trouble today," June assured her.

"But maybe Ira is. How many brothers and sisters do you have?" Mandy asked.

"Just my older brother. He's already finished school."

"You're lucky," Mandy said with a grin. To her relief, Ira was waiting at the door and Curtis was nowhere in sight.

When Mandy and Ira arrived at the farm, they saw Aunt Bess digging beside the front porch. She'd uncovered the roots of a dead shrub and was trying to pull it loose. She saw the two of them and called. "After you change your clothes, I want you to give me a hand here."

There she goes again, Mandy thought, never asking, always demanding. In silent rebellion, Mandy took her time changing her clothes, hoping Aunt Bess and Ira would finish without her. When she came out a little later, they were still at work.

"Mandy, you take the shovel and pry from that side, and we'll pull in this direction," Aunt Bess directed.

As Mandy pushed on the handle, she saw a long root running straight down into the ground. The shrub would never let go until that was severed. She jammed the shovel downward, and its sharp edge sliced cleanly through the root. The shrub's sudden release sent Ira and Aunt Bess sprawling backward. Dirt spattered them, leaving wet, clinging globs on their faces and their clothes. Mandy burst out laughing, and Ira scrambled to his feet, laughing too.

"There's nothing funny about an old woman falling down on the cold ground," Aunt Bess declared.

"Oh, Aunt Bess, you're not old," Ira said, grinning and reaching a hand to help her up.

She rose to her feet, her lips puckered with disapproval. "There's another dead shrub on the far side of of the steps," she said, and waved a hand at the shovel Mandy was holding. Mandy had other things to do—homework, getting the sheep—but she didn't have the nerve to cross Aunt Bess.

"Why don't you ever use the front porch, Aunt Bess?" Ira asked.

"I misplaced the front door key several years ago," she replied. "I'll probably come across it some day, but until then, I get along fine without a front porch."

"Dad says every house should have a front porch," Ira went on. "Isn't that right, Mandy?"

Mandy didn't answer or even look up. She just kept jabbing the shovel into the soft, wet earth. Why did Ira have to talk about him as if he was still alive?

"Your father was a smart man," Aunt Bess said. Her tone and her words said he was dead, though Ira didn't seem to notice. Mandy didn't look at either of them, but continued her relentless digging around the second shrub.

In the weeds by the porch steps, Ira uncovered a clump of daffodils. "Mrs. Nichols said we're going to draw flowers tomorrow."

"Maybe you'd like to take some of these with you," Aunt Bess said. When he nodded, she went on. "Any more trouble from the eighth grader?"

"Nope." Ira shook his head. "Tappy and me

played ball both recesses, and he never even came near us."

Aunt Bess stopped pulling on the shrub and faced him, her hands on her hips. "There's only one way to handle a bully, and that's stand up to him."

"I know," Ira said, "but Mama doesn't want us to fight."

"Sometimes you have to fight, whether or not you want to," she responded. "That's why we went to war. We had to."

In the uneasy silence that followed, Aunt Bess and Mandy looked at each other and, for a moment, their minds seemed to meet on the same sad thought. Mandy had always assumed that the government made her father go to war. She'd never considered that he might have gone to fight because he thought it was the right thing to do. A bitterness welled up in her that she could almost taste. What did it matter now why he went?

As she stared off across the valley, Aunt Bess spoke in a good-humored tone Mandy had never heard before. "I think I'll go in and make some popcorn. Can you finish getting this old shrub out of here, Ira?"

"Sure," he said with a grin. "I'll just pretend it's Curtis Jones and yank it into next week."

"Good," Aunt Bess said. "By the time Mandy

brings in the sheep, the popcorn should be ready."

Mandy started for the pasture, unwilling to be drawn into their lighthearted plans. She ached with thoughts of her father, longing for him and wishing for what she knew she could never have again.

chapter ❧ seven

*M*andy hurried across the pasture, trying to out-distance her painful thoughts, but she could not escape them. The loneliness, the loss clung to her, as the dead shrubs had clung to the soggy earth. If only there was someone to talk to, someone who understood how she felt.

Mandy remembered talking to her mother a few days after they'd received word of her father's death.

"Life will be empty without him," her mother had said. The words had proved true. Inside Mandy there seemed to be a great, black void that threatened to swallow up the memory of her father. Each day that passed, his image became more shadowy, more indistinct. They just had to get the Fulton place. Mandy knew she would be close to him there.

Mandy found herself among the sheep before she knew it. She was grateful for the distraction. They surrounded her, looking for the food she'd forgotten to bring. She turned for the barn and walked most of the way in the midst of the milling flock. Dean had said the sheep were more afraid of her than she was of them, but they didn't look afraid. Their black eyes followed her, soft, lustrous eyes that seemed to shine with trust. She hadn't thought of it before, but the sheep depended on her. She could see their faith in her, never doubting that she would give them what they needed. It made Mandy feel guilty. She hadn't earned that kind of trust.

When Mandy entered the kitchen, she saw Ira and Aunt Bess sitting by the table, their heads bent close together over something in Aunt Bess's lap. Mandy slipped off her coat and went to see what they were doing.

"Look at this, Mandy," Ira said. He pointed to the pieces of red crepe paper spread across Aunt Bess's apron. As Mandy watched, Aunt Bess picked up her scissors and, using her thumb and one flat blade, stretched the outer edge of each paper until it curled over the steel. Then she gathered the dainty, rounded petals together. Fascinated, Mandy drew in her breath and held it while Aunt Bess's gnarled hands shaped the papers into an elegant rose.

"You see this, Ira," Aunt Bess said, leaning over so he could look down into the flower's heart. "The petals overlap at the base. Remember that when you're drawing tomorrow."

"Can I take this to school?" Ira almost whispered.

Without speaking, Aunt Bess bound the flower together at the bottom with a thin wire, then handed it to him.

"Where did you learn to do that?" Mandy asked.

"My grandmother taught me when I was about your age," she said, glancing up at Mandy. "I haven't made any for years. I'm surprised I even remember how. Seeing the daffodils reminded me."

"It's just . . . just beautiful," Mandy said, then startled even herself with her next words. "Do you think I could learn to do it?"

Aunt Bess's thoughtful gaze settled on Mandy. "If I can do it with these old hands, you can." She went over and opened the oven door, pulled out a dishpan of steamy, golden popcorn, and carried it to the table. It was several minutes before anyone spoke; they were too busy eating.

"You'll see Dean tomorrow at school, won't you?" Aunt Bess asked Mandy.

"If he's there," Mandy said. "I think he only comes when he feels like it."

"Ask him to come by, will you? The corn sheller needs fixing."

"Sure," Mandy replied. "He's looking for work." He was serious about getting some sheep, Mandy knew. Why else would he work all day on the fences? She wondered just how much of the thirty dollars he'd saved. She had more than that upstairs in her dresser drawer, but it wouldn't be spent on anything as unimportant as a sheep.

After supper, Mandy and Ira bent over their homework at the kitchen table, while Aunt Bess washed the supper dishes. Mandy read and reread the Gettysburg Address until even the long words became familiar. The better she understood it, the more she hated it, the talk of war and of dying. She had to memorize it, but as soon as she recited it for Mr. Mills, she intended to forget it.

She recalled Dean's flawless recital. Suddenly it came to her how he'd been able to learn it in just one evening. Since this was his second year in the seventh grade, he'd just reviewed what he'd learned last year. And she'd thought he was so smart!

Mandy was trying to write down the Gettysburg Address from memory when her mother came home. Before she had even shed her coat, Ira called to her.

"Look at this, Mama," he said, holding out the red paper rose. "Aunt Bess made it."

"It's beautiful. I remember trying to make paper flowers when I stayed here, but I could never quite get them right." She got the plate of food that Aunt Bess had kept warm for her and took a seat at the table, then glanced over at Mandy. "How did school go today?"

"Curtis didn't bother me or Ira," Mandy replied.

"That's good," her mother said. "I hope there won't be any more problems. I've got enough on my mind with the store."

"Wasn't this the day Mr. Armstrong was going to the hospital?" Aunt Bess asked.

"Yes, he went this afternoon. They'll operate tomorrow morning."

Mandy suddenly realized that she had a very special interest in this man she'd never met. Mr. Armstrong's operation had to be a success, he had to get well. Only then could she get what she wanted.

"How long will Mr. Armstrong have to stay at home after the operation?" she asked her mother.

"There's no way of knowing for sure, but it will probably take several months. He's very sick."

When her mother's gaze rested on Mandy a long, unsettling time, Mandy murmured, "I was just wondering."

"I suspect you're more concerned about your own wants, Mandy, than you are about Mr. Armstrong's health."

"I don't even know him," Mandy mumbled and rose to her feet. She slammed her books together and headed for the stairs. She had a right to be concerned about Mr. Armstrong's health. What happened to him had a lot to do with what happened to her. In fact, his health affected all of them.

It seemed that she and her mother could hardly talk anymore. They always ended up arguing. Her mother was so wrapped up in the store that she'd forgotten all about Garnet Creek. But I'll never forget, Mandy vowed.

The next day, before school started, Mandy delivered Aunt Bess's message to Dean. He told her he would come right after school. Evidently, he didn't have chores to do at home. Wait until he gets his sheep, Mandy thought. Then he'll have to go straight home every day after school. She'd already learned that animals needed to be looked after, even if you didn't do anything but just check to see that they were there.

Mandy was talking to Ira during recess when she saw his gaze shift suddenly to something just over her shoulder. A sharp tug on her braid caused her head to jerk backward, and she spun around, angry and on guard. A short distance away, Curtis stood untangling the knot of her green hair ribbon. He smoothed it between his fingers, then tied it to one of his shirt buttons. Without looking at her, he turned and walked away.

Anger bubbled like boiling water inside of Mandy. It was no use trying to get the ribbon from Curtis. She probably couldn't even catch him. She thought of a dozen different names to call him, each one worse than the last. It didn't help get her ribbon back, but it made her feel better. Just then a hand touched her shoulder. It was June.

"He's just awful," June said. "The worst thing is, I think he likes you."

"Likes me! Well, I hate him," Mandy said, jerking away. Not only did she hate Curtis, she hated everything and everyone in Parrish Grove.

When Mrs. Nichols's bell sounded the end of recess, Mandy was the last to climb the fire escape steps at the back of the building. Everyone was already at work when she entered the classroom. Though Mr. Mills's eyes followed her down the aisle, he remained silent.

As she slid into her seat, Mandy was astonished to see her hair ribbon curled in a neat circle on her desktop. Her angry gaze slid across to Curtis. With an arm hiding most of his face, he appeared deeply engrossed in his English book.

Mandy tied the ribbon around her braid, silently renewing her vow to leave this place. She would find a way to get them back to Garnet Creek if it was her final act on earth.

The school day dragged to a close, and Dean joined Mandy as she waited for Ira on the front steps. When they started for home, Mandy saw Curtis standing by himself in the school yard, not doing anything, just watching them go. It was a kind of sweet revenge to ignore him.

Dean and Ira walked along, talking about a buzzard circling overhead. Finally, Dean spoke to Mandy.

"Have you learned the Gettysburg Address?" he asked.

"Not all of it," Mandy said.

"There are only ten sentences, but the last one's a lulu." He grinned at her. "It has eighty-three words."

"Lincoln made the war sound like something

good," Mandy declared. "But war's not good, it's awful. It's *hell.*"

"Mandy! Mama would skin you alive if she heard you cussing," Ira said.

"Well, it's true," she said. Avoiding Dean's curious gaze, she stared across the fields. If she looked at him, the smoldering anger might come gushing out. The words were there, pushing ever nearer the surface: Yes, war killed my father and a part of me too.

"She's right, Ira," Dean said. "War is hell."

"Our dad went to war," Ira said.

A choked sound escaped Mandy's lips and she kicked a stone and sent it spinning down the lane ahead of them. Ira shouldn't talk to strangers about their father. They wouldn't understand; they wouldn't even care.

"Look there," Dean said, pointing toward a tree whose branches hung over the stream by the lane. A bluish gray bird sat on a limb above the water, its throat dazzling white against the tree's green leaves.

"What is it?" Ira asked.

"A kingfisher," Dean replied. "It's looking for minnows."

Suddenly, the squatty bird fell from the branch, its short beak aimed at the water. It hit with a splash, then, moments later, fluttered up to the branch again, its beak empty.

While the boys stopped to watch the bird, Mandy walked on to the house. She was thankful Dean hadn't asked any questions about their father. Ira might have blurted out the whole, horrible story.

Aunt Bess was in the kitchen when she entered. "Dean's here," she said.

Aunt Bess wiped her hands on a towel and started for the door. "Oh, Mandy, I need your help with something. Come out to the barn after you've changed clothes."

Walking toward the barn a few minutes later, Mandy saw Dean through the open granary door, already at work on the corn sheller. Ira was with him, holding onto the sheller's big iron wheel with both hands.

Mandy strolled into the barn and as soon as she entered, Aunt Bess called out an order.

"Bring one of those lambs out here," she said, waving a hand toward the back barn door.

Knowing better than to ask any questions, Mandy did as she was told. She tried to catch one of the lambs by reaching over the gate, but they both shied away behind their mother.

"Easy, Mildred," she murmured as she straddled the gate. Inside the pen, she cornered one of the lambs and picked it up. "You know me," she whispered. "I carried you all the way home the other day." With the lamb as helpless as a baby in her arms, she passed through the empty barn and out into the afternoon sunlight.

Aunt Bess was waiting beside a thick, square

block of wood smoothed and gray with age. She held a hatchet in one hand and a hammer in the other. Mandy's chest tightened. Was she going to kill the lamb?

Without offering any explanation, Aunt Bess motioned for Mandy to set the lamb's rump down on top of the block.

"Now," she said, "hold it up against you so that it can't move."

Mandy grabbed the lamb's front legs with her left hand and positioned its back against her as she'd seen Dean do up on the hill.

"Here, hold its back legs too," Aunt Bess ordered.

Clasping the back legs with her right hand, Mandy had the sinking feeling that she was about to be an accomplice to a cold-blooded murder. Her heartbeat faded away to nothing.

Aunt Bess bent down and spread the lamb's tail flat on the wooden block. Then she placed the hatchet blade across the tail about an inch from the lamb's body. For a brief moment, she balanced the hammer head against the head of the hatchet. When Mandy saw the hammer rising, she squeezed her eyes shut, but she could still hear and feel the solid blow. The lamb jumped at the moment of impact, then lay perfectly still. Even before she looked, Mandy knew that the tail had been cut off.

Aunt Bess's matter-of-fact voice broke through

the fog in Mandy's mind. "Hold it steady so I can put some disinfectant on it," she said. She brushed the separated tail off the block, and it fell to the ground like a soggy mitten.

Mandy felt her stomach turn over and something bitter rose in her throat. She closed her eyes again rather than watch Aunt Bess pour the dark medicine on what was left of the lamb's tail.

"Are you all right?" Aunt Bess asked. Mandy nodded, unable to face the penetrating gaze.

"This is necessary, Mandy. The tails get dirty and make a good breeding place for insects. Once that happens, they become infected and have to come off anyway. So it's just better to remove them before they get infected." She scratched one of the lamb's ears. "Now, take this one inside and bring out the other one."

A wail threatened to come screeching out of Mandy's throat, but she fought it down. Gritting her teeth, she carried the lamb back to the barn and lifted it into the pen. She considered just walking out and letting Aunt Bess do her dirty work alone. But despite the weakness in her knees, something in her wanted to prove her toughness, her strength in the face of Aunt Bess's unfeeling brutality. She picked up the other lamb and carried it outside.

Rather than watch the procedure again, Mandy stared at Aunt Bess's face. The high, sharp cheekbones and thin lips gave her face a kind of stark cruelty, though her eyes were clear and tranquil, even as she brought the hammer down.

After returning the second lamb to its mother, Mandy went out through the barnyard gate and headed for the pasture. She'd forgotten to bring grain for the sheep, but she wasn't going back for it. She needed fresh air and clean, wide spaces to clear away the sickening shock of what she'd witnessed.

At first, she kept the gruesome thoughts at bay by repeating the Gettysburg Address out loud. Once she reached the crest of the hill, she paused to look down on Aunt Bess's farm. From this distance, the ordeal was almost bearable. Aunt Bess had said it was necessary. And the way she'd done it was skillful and quick and neat, Mandy had to admit. Still, she was relieved it was all over.

Seeing the flock grazing along the back side of the hill, Mandy called to them. They came, the yearlings in front, the slower, heavier ewes lumbering along behind. As she watched the sluggish ewes, the awful truth slowly filled her mind until she groaned aloud. The two lambs in the barn were just the beginning. There must be at least thirty ewes here ready to have their lambs, and every one of those lambs would have a tail.

chapter ✣ eight

At Aunt Bess's urging, Dean stayed and ate supper with them. After washing his hands at the sink, he took a chair next to Ira. Mandy was carrying a plate of bread to the table when her mother came through the door.

"Am I too late?" she asked, slipping off her coat.

"No, no," Aunt Bess said. "We have one extra but there's plenty of food." When everyone was seated, she resumed her conversation with Dean.

"Could you come by Friday after school?" she asked him.

"Sure. Something else need fixing?"

"No, Ned McGuire is going to shear the sheep that day. I thought you could come and help stack the wool in that empty stall in the barn."

"I'll be here," Dean said.

"You still planning to get a ewe?" Aunt Bess asked.

"I have to hang a gate before I'll be ready for her," Dean said. "I don't have all the money yet, but I'll be over one of these days to pick out one."

"Don't forget," Aunt Bess said, "you'll have to get some grain. Coming up to lambing, the ewe needs to be well fed. And afterward too."

"I know," Dean replied. "And that takes money. A few more days' work ought to do it, though."

"The corn sheller's fixed," Ira broke in. "It just needed a cog wheel tightened."

"Good," Aunt Bess replied. "After supper you can shell some corn for the sheep."

"I thought looking after the sheep was Mandy's job," Ira said.

"It is," Aunt Bess said, "but shelling the corn is yours."

Ira grinned at her. "I'll make some sheep corn if you'll make some popcorn."

Aunt Bess did not reply but leaned back in her chair and gazed across at Ira. Despite her customary frown, Mandy saw the veiled laughter in her eyes. Aunt Bess liked Ira.

"Do you do any painting?" Mandy's mother asked Dean.

Dean laid his loaded fork back on his plate. "I've done some," he said, and seemed to hold his breath at the prospect of another job.

"The benches outside the store need to be painted, and the front door too. Would you have time?"

"I could do it Saturday, if it doesn't rain," he said.

"Good. We'll expect you about ten o'clock."

"I can help him," Ira said.

"No, I'll need you and Mandy to help Stella in the store while I'm in Garnet Creek."

"Oh, Mama, you're going to Garnet Creek!" Mandy said. "Can I go along?"

"No, Mandy, you can't. I'm riding with someone else and I have some business to take care of. I may not even have time to visit Grandma Gates."

"What business, Mama?"

"We'll talk about it later, Mandy."

Mandy hung her head, longing for the only place she could think of as home. She belonged in Garnet Creek; her friends were there, everything she wanted was there.

Lost in her rambling thoughts, Mandy hardly noticed when Dean got up to leave, and Aunt Bess and Ira followed him outside. Her mother's voice finally brought her to attention.

"Mandy, I want to talk to you about Garnet Creek . . . and about the store."

The strangeness in her mother's voice made Mandy turn and look at her more closely. In that moment, her mother's eyes reminded her of the newborn lambs, of their mute, feeble pleading for mercy, for acceptance.

"It could be that our plans might be changed . . ." When she hesitated, Mandy rushed to finish the thought with her own yearning hope.

"You mean we might move back to Garnet Creek sooner than we thought. Oh, I hope we can, Mama. That would be just . . ."

"No, that isn't what I meant . . ."

"We can stay with Grandma Gates until we talk to Mrs. Fulton," Mandy rattled on. "I'll finally get away from . . ."

Her mother interrupted her. "Stop it, Mandy. Just stop it!" Her eyes blazed, then the light died and she propped her elbows on the table, covering her face with her hands.

Mandy stared at the rigid, hunched shoulders and hoped her mother wouldn't cry. She'd seen her mother cry before. There were plenty of tears after her father's death, sudden tears that caught them all unaware, more often quiet tears in quiet moments. She'd seen her mother's tears spill over, like water over a too full dam. Only one time had Mandy seen the dam break.

She'd been sweeping the kitchen and thought she was alone until she heard an odd sound. She spun around. Her mother was sitting on the edge of a chair, staring down at her hands. Stretched between her fingers was a black, ragged shoelace. Mandy knew at once it had belonged to her father. Tears streamed down her mother's face and fell on her clenched hands.

What scared Mandy the most was the way her

mother had rocked back and forth, back and forth, in a slow, anguished rhythm. It was that terrible, soundless rocking that had sent Mandy running, not to her mother but away from her, in a desperate attempt to flee the fear and the pain.

Her mother's tired voice broke the spell of the nightmare memory. "I know it's hard in a new school, away from your friends."

Mandy felt a sharp stab of guilt. Her mother was only trying to take care of them. "I'm sorry, Mama. It's hard on you too, working all the time." Her mother's face softened into a smile.

"What was it you started to say before?" Mandy asked.

"We can talk about it some other time, Mandy, sometime when I'm not so tired."

The rest of the week seemed to pass in a flurry of activities. Mandy recited the Gettysburg Address on Friday. Rather than standing by her seat, Mr. Mills called her up to his desk. She stood with her back to the other students, her gaze riveted on George Washington's picture, pulling her braid over her shoulder and twisting the ribbon as she spoke. Coming to school that morning, she'd said it perfectly to Ira, but Mr. Mills had to prompt her twice.

Several persons brought money for the map and dropped it into the green jar. At every recess a few curious students wandered by the desk to gaze at the meager pile of coins in the bottom. Mr. Mills still used the green jar for a bell, but the coins had dulled its clear, silver tone.

At Friday morning recess, June and Mandy, along with some of the eighth grade boys, watched Mr. Mills dump out the coins and count them. He reported a total of $2.38, then dribbled them back into the jar. Picking up a pencil, he tapped the glass. "When it gets full," he said, "it won't ring at all. I guess I should be looking for another jar."

Mandy drew in a breath and then spoke up. "Why don't you get a rope," she began, but as all eyes turned on her, the sentence seemed to falter and fall apart. ". . . For the bell . . . up in the . . ."

Mr. Mills's gaze rested on her, making her even more uncomfortable. "I'd forgotten about that bell," he said.

"They sell rope down at Armstrong's store," Curtis spoke up. For an instant, his eyes slid over to Mandy, then bounced back to Mr. Mills.

"Let's take a look," Mr. Mills said, moving toward the cloakroom. June and Mandy stood just outside the door and watched as one boy was lifted into the small, square opening in the ceiling. A moment later there was a clang, then the boy reappeared. "It still works."

"I'll get a piece of rope," Mr. Mills said. "Fifteen feet should do it."

"Who's going to ring the bell?" Curtis asked.

"I think it would be best to take turns, have a different person every day," Mr. Mills said.

"But who's going to go first?" Curtis persisted.

Mr. Mills walked past the girls and over to his desk before answering. "I think Mandy should go first, since it was her idea."

Mandy went to her seat with a red face. She had no desire to be first, or to be singled out for any special rewards. Well, she'd do it. It would be easier to ring the bell than to argue about it.

Dean came to school at noon, clad in ragged trousers and a faded flannel shirt. Mandy guessed he was dressed for his after-school job with Aunt Bess.

There was a pickup truck out by the barn when the three of them arrived at the farm, and Dean confirmed that it belonged to Ned McGuire. He went on to the barn while Mandy and Ira hurried in to change clothes. They'd never watched a sheep shearer before and were eager to see him in action.

When they got to the barn, Dean was already at work carrying tied fleeces into the unused horse stall. Mandy counted seven sheep still confined in the barn, awaiting their turn. Through the open door, she caught a glimpse of the newly sheared sheep in the back lot, their bodies creamy white and all angles and sharp edges.

Aunt Bess introduced Mandy and Ira to Mr. McGuire. A tall, smiling man in dirty overalls, he paused only a moment to nod a greeting. "Just call me Ned," he said, then turned back to the ewe between his knees.

The cement floor had been swept clean where Ned worked, although tufts of wool skittered around his feet as he moved. Once he'd clipped off the heavy tags of wool hanging down from the ewe's body, he upended her and set her down on her hindquarters, with her back resting against his legs. Her round, full belly stuck out like a fuzzy balloon.

Beginning under the chin, Ned clipped the wool close to the sheep's body, working down over the swollen belly. The fleece fell away, exposing the inner wool, fluffy and clean and white. Rolling the animal to the right, then left, he cut the sides and up over the back.

When he finished, he set the ewe on her feet, then led her out through the door to a long, metal tank filled with a white liquid. Mandy and Ira followed him, curious about what he was going to do. To their amazement, he picked up the ewe and set her down in the tank until every part except her head was submerged.

Being careful to keep the animal's nose out of the bath, Ned held her there for a minute or so, then squeezing her nostrils tight, he pushed her head under. When he let her up, she blinked her eyes several times to clear away the liquid. Ned ducked her head under a second time, then lifted her out on the ground. The ewe trotted away towards the grazing flock without looking back.

"What is that? It smells bad." Ira wrinkled his nose.

"It's a dip that gets rid of ticks and lice," Ned told him. "It smells bad but it works good."

The sun was setting when Ned finished with the last ewe. After transferring the pungent dip to a barrel in the back of the truck, he gathered up the rest of his equipment and left.

While Dean and Ira carried off the rest of the fleeces, Aunt Bess and Mandy coaxed the sheep back into the barn and fed them. They looked clean but naked, and somehow vulnerable with their skinny legs and black, glittering eyes. The pungent odor of the dip filled every part of the barn.

"Can you stay for supper?" Aunt Bess asked Dean.

"No, my mom's expecting me home," he said.

"Well, don't leave yet. I'll send Ira back with your pay." She motioned Ira to follow her. Ira returned shortly and handed Dean two folded dollar bills.

"Thanks," Dean said, looking pleased as he slid the money into his pocket.

"Don't thank me," Ira said. "I'm just a delivery boy. My next delivery is an armload of wood." And he took off for the house again.

Dean followed Mandy over to Mildred's pen. The

lambs were having supper too, one on each side of their mother, their cropped tails still black with disinfectant.

"I hope the ewe I get has twins," Dean said.

Smiling at the lambs' eagerness, Mandy asked, "What made you decide to start a sheep herd?"

"I've been helping your Aunt Bess with hers for a couple of years, and I've learned to like them. They're easy to handle, easy to get along with."

"Yes." Mandy smiled at him. "All they want is something to eat and a place to get in out of the rain."

Dean smiled back, then leaned forward and rested his arms on the wooden gate. "Everyone should have something to work for, a dream they can make happen."

Mandy pushed her hands deep in her pockets and closed her eyes, letting her mind spin across the miles to Garnet Creek. As if she were right there, she could see the Fulton place, its high gables and spacious front porch. It would be a beautiful place to live. "I've got a dream . . ." She stopped and opened her eyes. Had she spoken out loud? Dean was looking at her with a faint smile.

"That makes two of us," was all he said, and he rose to his full height so that his eyes were level with hers. Then he reached over and plucked a wisp of hay out of her hair. It was so quiet Mandy could hear the sucking lambs in the darkness. She felt a throbbing inside, an intense longing to tell

Dean all about her father and the Fulton place.

He already knew her father had gone to war; Ira had made sure of that. But he knew nothing of the Fulton place. He probably wouldn't understand anyway, how she needed the Fulton place to bring her father close. Dean still had his father. How could he know the sudden panic Mandy felt when she couldn't even remember her father's face.

Strangely breathless, she followed Dean through the barn door, wanting to talk to him but unable to lift her secret into the light. With a parting wave, he disappeared into the night, leaving Mandy alone with her aching heart.

chapter ❧ nine

*T*he next morning, Mandy and Ira set out for the store as soon as they'd finished breakfast. Ira danced in the sunlight, chasing a toad into the weeds, throwing a stone at a noisy crow.

Mandy walked with her head down, unmindful of his bubbling spirits. She was remembering how she'd wanted to talk to Dean about her father. If he'd asked, she would have told him everything, how she missed her father, how he was gradually slipping away from her, why it was so important for her to live at the Fulton place. Maybe it was better that he hadn't asked. She didn't want him to know all that about her. She didn't want any strings tying her to this place.

When they arrived at the store, their mother was standing at the front door, waiting for her ride.

"Go see Stella, Mandy. She'll show you and Ira what to do. I'll be back this afternoon."

"What are you going to do in Garnet Creek?" Mandy asked. Her mother had never explained the reason for her trip.

There was an awkward silence, then her mother said, "I got a letter from Mrs. Fulton . . ."

"Mrs. Fulton!" Mandy almost shouted. "She's going to sell her place, isn't she? Oh, Mama, tell her we'll buy it . . . please!"

"Mandy, everything's changed since we talked about buying her property. And I have a commitment now, to Mr. Armstrong . . ."

"That's not important," Mandy broke in. "The important thing is getting the Fulton place." She stopped and looked around. Although the store was empty of customers, Ira and Stella were at the cash register, only a few steps away. Mandy lowered her voice and edged closer to her mother. She had to explain about her father's fading image. "Mama, you don't know what it's like . . ."

Her mother interrupted, her eyes flashing, her voice hoarse with anger. "I know what it's like to be left without a husband, and with two children to take care of. You'll never understand that, Mandy."

With those stinging words, she brushed past Mandy and out the front door. When a car pulled up moments later, she got in and rode off without looking at Mandy again.

Loneliness sliced at Mandy like an icy wind, leaving her cold and shivery and on the verge of tears. She sat at the counter brooding for several minutes before she was able to force herself to go and help Stella and Ira.

Stella showed her how to record purchases on the regular customers' charge pads, and how to ring up cash sales on the cash register. She had to admit that she liked being behind the counter. She and Ira were playing store again, but this time they sold real products and received real money.

When the store was empty of customers, Mandy helped Ira unpack canned goods and stack them on the shelves. A ladder, made to slide along a metal guide up close to the ceiling, gave them access to the highest shelves. Ira seemed to like those top shelves best.

The next person to enter the store was Dean, right on time. Mandy noticed for the first time how skinny he was, how his shoulders curved forward around his flat chest. His bare arms were thin and angular, like branches on a young tree. He looked as though he didn't get enough to eat. Mandy remembered what Aunt Bess had said about his mother. Surely the woman must cook once in a while.

Stella came from the back of the store, carrying a bucket of paint and a brush. "You're looking for these, I guess," she said to Dean.

"Yeah." He reached for them. "Do you know if she wants the boards behind the bench painted too?"

"Let me take a look," Stella said, and they went out together.

Mandy watched them from inside. He and Stella acted like friends, and it made Mandy wonder what

Stella would do if she caught Dean stealing something. For that matter, Mandy wondered what she would do if she saw him take something from the store. She hoped she wouldn't have to face that problem today.

At noon, Mandy and Ira perched on stools at the ice cream counter to eat their lunch, while Stella stood by the window where she could observe the gas pumps. Dean joined them, leaning against the counter as relaxed as though he'd known Mandy and Ira all his life. He had flecks of green paint on his face and hands, and one large glob in his hair. When Ira followed Stella out to the gas pumps, Dean turned to Mandy. "June says we're getting a rope for the school bell."

Mandy nodded, wondering if he knew she'd suggested it. His next comment revealed he knew all about it.

"And you get to ring it first," he said.

"You can do it if you want," she said with a wry smile.

"And make everyone late for school?" he said, grinning. After a while he went on. "I've been trying to think of some way for us to make money for the map fund. Any ideas?"

Mandy shook her head. She'd forgotten all about it. She didn't care about the wall map any more than she cared about the bell. The only reason she'd mentioned a rope for the bell was because there were a few basics every school should have, and a bell was one of them.

In early afternoon, Mandy saw a pickup truck pull in beside the gas pumps. A white-faced calf swayed in the back, trying to maintain its balance in the unsteady truck bed. As the truck rolled to a stop, a familiar figure rose up beside the calf. It was June, her hair in pigtails. When she climbed over the tailgate and dropped to the ground, Mandy went to meet her.

"Where you headed?" Mandy asked.

"Dad is taking this calf to a man over on Sheets Ridge. I was just riding along. What are you doing here?"

"Mama went away for the day so Ira and I are working in the store."

Just then, a man appeared at the side of the truck and tugged on the calf's rope to make sure it was still tied. He looked at the girls and smiled, and his round face was wrinkled and kind.

"Mandy, this is my dad," June said. She stepped over beside him and linked her arm in his.

Mandy nodded to him, thinking how much June looked like her father.

"Dad, can I stay here with Mandy while you deliver the calf?" June asked, looking up at him.

"Well, sure. If it's all right with Mandy."

"Oh, yes," Mandy said at once. "She can help me in the store."

The girls sidestepped Dean's wet paint and passed inside the store. Once behind the counter, they leaned across it, waiting for someone to come in.

"Why do I have to do all the work?" Ira called down from his perch on the ladder.

"We're working," Mandy replied, grinning at June.

"Yes, waiting is the hardest work of all," June added.

They didn't have to wait long. A rush of customers soon had them all busy. While Mandy recorded the purchases and figured prices, June collected the goods. They finally called Ira down to help them because he knew where everything was located.

A little later, a truck pulled up in front of the store, with dozens of cases of soda stacked on the flat bed. The driver carried several cases inside, then, one at a time, placed the bottles in the cooler, leaving only the caps visible above the crushed ice.

Dean followed the driver inside, carrying his paint bucket and brush. Mandy heard him and Stella talking, and saw Stella hand him some money. He folded the bills and slipped them in his pocket, then raised a hand in farewell to the girls and left.

Mandy nudged June and pointed to Dean heading straight for the beverage truck. He lifted a bottle of soda from its rack, then levered it against the wooden case to pry off the cap. Without even a glance in the direction of the store, he tipped it up and drank as he strolled out of sight around the store building.

Mandy glanced over at the truck driver, still at work filling the cooler. He hadn't noticed, and even seemed unconcerned about the unguarded truck. With all those bottles in easy reach, maybe he was used to finding one missing now and then.

"Stella told me he takes things," Mandy whispered.

"It's mostly just little things, nothing valuable," June said. "His family's poor."

Just because his family was poor didn't give him the right to steal, Mandy thought. She wondered how he'd like it if someone stole something from him.

Shortly after June left with her father, Mandy's mother returned from Garnet Creek. Mandy wanted to ask about Mrs. Fulton, but her mother looked grim and unapproachable. Besides, Mandy was still smarting from their earlier argument.

On the way home, Ira ran ahead, leaving Mandy and her mother walking side by side. Finally her mother broke the silence. "You were right, Mandy. Mrs. Fulton wants to sell her house. She's moving in with her daughter."

"What did you tell her?" Mandy asked, hardly breathing.

"I told her . . ." She paused, then continued in a softer tone. "Mandy, I not only went to see Mrs. Fulton, I also went to the bank. I wanted to find out about a loan."

"You mean we're going to buy the Fulton place?" Mandy's sudden happiness made her bounce upward on her toes.

"Wait, Mandy, you're always jumping ahead."

Her mother was no longer looking at her and Mandy felt her breath catch in her throat. There was something wrong, something frightening in her mother's voice.

"Mr. Armstrong has decided to retire, and he's offered to sell the store to me . . . to us."

"What!" Mandy came to a halt, her mouth falling open. "You can't, Mama," she got out at last. "We're going back to Garnet Creek in the fall. You said we were."

"I know what we planned, but . . ."

"We're going to buy the Fulton place." Mandy's voice rose in anger. "We're going to have a real home, just like Dad wanted." She glared at her mother, but she was seeing her father's smiling face. Several moments passed before she realized her mother was talking.

"So if we owned the store, we could move into that little house behind the store building where Mr. Armstrong lived. That's one of the good things about it. Not only would we get the store, but we'd get a home along with it."

"But you don't have enough money to buy a store," Mandy said, clutching at any thin straw.

"There's the money we've been saving for a home.

Mr. Armstrong said if I make a good down payment, I can pay off the rest in monthly installments."

"Mama, you can't spend that money we saved for the Fulton place. It wouldn't be right."

Her mother laid an arm across Mandy's shoulders, urging her on down the road. "Mrs. Fulton's house is just a place to live, but the store is a home and a job," she said in a quiet voice.

Mandy reached up and pushed her mother's arm away, then walked on alone. She didn't even look up when her mother came alongside.

"I know how you feel, Mandy, and I haven't decided anything yet. I wanted to talk to you and Ira first. And to Aunt Bess."

"What business is it of hers?" Mandy demanded.

"She's lived in this community all her life. And she's known Mr. Armstrong for years."

Mandy walked on, not even listening anymore. There was nothing left for them to say to one another. Her mother had turned against her, and against her father too.

At the supper table, Mandy picked at her food and listened to her mother and Aunt Bess talk about buying the store. Ira didn't seem the least bit upset about the plan, which depressed Mandy even more. She'd hoped he would be her ally, help pressure their mother into giving up the idea.

Finally, wanting to get away, she excused herself and went outside. There'd been no time to get the sheep before supper, and the sun was already low in the west. As she passed the front porch, she noticed that the weeds had been cleaned away from either side of the steps and geraniums planted next to the daffodils. If Aunt Bess was trying to make the place more homey just for them, she needn't bother. They weren't going to be there for long. Besides, they couldn't use the porch anyway. Aunt Bess didn't even have a key to the front door.

It's none of my concern, Mandy thought. No matter where they moved to, she'd be glad to leave here. No more Aunt Bess and no more sheep. There wasn't one thing she'd miss about this place.

From the lower pasture, Mandy saw the sheep on top of the hill, and paused to call them. "Whoooee . . ." They started down and soon the hillside swarmed with the white animals. They looked pitifully small, she thought, without their thick, gray coats of wool.

As the flock gathered around her, she counted and found three missing. Moments later, they appeared over the top of the hill and began their slow descent. Then Mandy spied the newborn lambs striving to keep up with their mothers. There were two sets of twins, and though their untried legs trembled, they managed to make their way down the slope. The last ewe paused near the top, looking down at Mandy, then back at her solitary lamb.

Mandy climbed up to them. The lamb seemed to

know what was expected and struggled to its feet, where it swayed on unsteady legs. The mother sheep nosed it, but when it took a step, it fell on its face and rolled several feet downhill.

Mandy picked it up, an arm under its neck, the other arm around its hindquarters, then headed toward the barn.

With the lambing season in full swing, surely Aunt Bess would keep the expectant ewes near the barn. Mandy ground her teeth together just thinking of all the lambs' tails to be cut off. But maybe she wouldn't have to help, if they moved . . . when they moved. Anyway, she didn't care what happened to the sheep. They were Aunt Bess's responsibility.

chapter ❦ *ten*

*M*andy was silent through breakfast the next morning, even refusing to speak when her mother braided her hair. She felt betrayed. On the way to school, her steps dragged as she pondered her mother's plan for buying the store. She had to figure out a way to stop it from happening.

Once in the classroom, Mandy was distracted by June's babbling excitement. June followed her into the cloakroom, then back to her seat, whispering behind her hands. "I have a great idea for making money for the map fund. But I want you to tell about it."

"Why me? It's your idea," Mandy said.

"Well, you suggested the bell rope and Mr. Mills liked that idea, so I thought . . ."

Mandy stopped June with a stare, her mind clouded with anger. I don't care whether they get a map or not, she said to herself. I'd like to forget the map and the bell and the whole darned school.

"Please, Mandy. Tell them about the box social."

"What's a box social?"

But June was already scurrying down the aisle to her desk as Mr. Mills signaled the beginning of the school day.

Through their arithmetic and science lessons, June kept looking back at Mandy with a pleading expression, her head bobbing the silent appeal. Just before recess, Mr. Mills called the entire room to attention.

"We'll take a few minutes to see if we can decide on a moneymaking project for our map purchase." He looked around the room but there was no immediate response. Then a hand went up in the fifth-grade row.

"Yes, Tommy. You have an idea."

Tommy, a skinny boy with unruly, brown hair and green eyes, blushed as he spoke. "We could sell night crawlers to the people goin' fishin' at the lake."

Ignoring the moans from the boys and the sounds of disgust from the girls, Mr. Mills went to the blackboard and wrote down Tommy's suggestion. Then he called on a sixth-grade girl who proposed they go around Parrish Grove and offer to wash people's windows. Other suggestions were added to the list: selling animal salve to farmers with livestock, raising a field of corn for a cash crop, gathering up scrap iron to sell for junk.

During the listing, June kept trying to prompt

Mandy to speak up. At last, when it seemed that all the plausible ideas had been posted, Mandy gave in and raised her hand.

"We could have a box social," she said.

There were murmurs across the room, hushed inquiries from the younger people, and, to Mandy's surprise, loud approval from the eighth-grade row.

"That's the best idea yet," she heard Curtis say.

She slid lower in her seat and tried to hide her reddening face. Curtis had backed her up when she mentioned getting a rope for the bell. Now he was doing it again. She had the sudden, revolting thought that he would probably have agreed to collecting snakes if she'd suggested it.

"Just a minute," Mr. Mills was saying. "Will someone explain just what a box social is?"

Mandy could feel his eyes on her but she refused to raise her head. She had no idea what it was; she'd never heard of a box social before. Moments passed, then Curtis spoke up.

"The girls . . . uh, the women fix a dinner for two people and put it in a box. Then the men bid on the boxes. Whoever bids the most money gets to eat with the girl . . . the woman."

"You forgot one important thing," came Dean's voice from the back of the room. Everyone swung around to look at him, even Mandy. "The boxes are decorated real pretty, with ribbons and flowers and bows, but no one knows whose box they've bought until it's all over."

So that's what happened at a box social, Mandy thought. It sounded awful. She slid around in her seat to see what Mr. Mills would do next.

He was standing by the list at the blackboard. "We'll vote on these, and the one with the highest number of votes will be our moneymaking project. Remember, you vote only once." He started down the list, counting the raised hands for each item and writing the number next to it.

Mandy watched as the first suggestions garnered only one or two votes. She heard Curtis tell the boy in front of him to put his hand down when selling salve was mentioned.

"Why? Everybody needs salve," Calhoun argued.

"People around here got enough salve to last them two lifetimes," Curtis muttered.

Calhoun dropped his hand and folded his arms as if he intended to give up voting altogether. But when Mr. Mills reached the last item on the list, the box social, Mandy saw Curtis punch the boy's shoulder. "Raise your hand, Calhoun, or else!"

The box social received the most, and most enthusiastic, votes. Mandy heard a girl across the room remark, "My dad always buys my box." Another girl chimed in, "My uncle buys mine."

Mandy hadn't thought of arranging for a relative

to buy the box. It would certainly be better than eating with a stranger. But I don't have an uncle, or a father, Mandy thought, and right then she decided she wouldn't bring a box. She didn't care whether they got a wall map or not. This wasn't her school.

They set the second Saturday in April as the date for the event. The boxes would be auctioned off, and sandwiches and lemonade would be sold to those who didn't buy a box. When everyone was finished eating, they would play a game of softball. Plans were made to publicize the social and try to get as many people involved as possible. The more boxes they sold, the more money they would take in.

Before dismissing them for recess, Mr. Mills pulled a rope from a desk drawer and asked the older boys to stay in and help him. He explained to everyone that if they got the rope attached, the big bell would ring at the end of recess.

From out in the classroom, Mandy and June watched two big boys lift Curtis up so that he could climb into the belfry.

"Curtis sure is enthused about the box social," June said. "I'll bet he's planning to buy your box."

"I'm not bringing a box," Mandy said.

"But . . . but . . ." June began. "If you're worried about who might get it, you can always tell someone how it's decorated, whoever you want to buy it."

"Is that what you do?" Mandy asked.

"Sure. My dad always buys mine, unless my brother, Danny, outbids him," June said, then grinned. "They're always fighting over my apple pie."

June was lucky, Mandy thought, to know for certain that someone in her family would buy her box. The only person Mandy had was Ira, and he was too little. Just the thought of having to share a box dinner with Curtis made Mandy's stomach turn over. Then she thought of Dean. He might be willing to buy her box, but where would he get the money? The safest plan was not to bring one.

"Please, Mandy. We could all eat together."

"I'll think about it," Mandy said, but she was already certain that her answer would be no.

Mr. Mills and the eighth-grade boys were still gazing up at the cloakroom ceiling. The dangling rope twisted and danced in their midst, and once there was a dull clang from above. At last Curtis's legs dropped through the hole, and the boys grabbed him and lowered him to the floor.

"That's a good job, boys," Mr. Mills said. With one hand clasping the rope, he looked at his watch. "And just in time." Gazing out into the classroom, he beckoned to Mandy. "It's time to ring the bell," he said.

As she approached, the boys pushed back against the wall to make room for her. "How long should I ring it?" she asked Mr. Mills.

"Well, I think you should ring it long enough and loud enough for the whole community to hear it."

Mandy felt a strong resistance to her first tug so she grabbed the rope in both hands and pulled down hard. A clear knell sounded above her, then her hands jerked upward with the bell's rebound. She pulled again and again, and her measured motion set off a thrilling, reverberating peal. She hadn't realized that ringing the bell would be fun. She continued pulling as the boys went to raise the windows and listen to the open-air sound. Finally, Mr. Mills nodded to her from his desk.

When Mandy came out of the cloakroom, June started clapping and soon everyone else joined in, including Mr. Mills. Mandy made a face at June as she hurried to her seat. She knew they were not applauding her so much as the restored bell, but it embarrassed her just the same. She was thankful when Mr. Mills set everyone to work.

As soon as Mandy and Ira got home, Ira told Aunt Bess about the upcoming event to raise money for a map. "We're going to have a boxing social."

"A box social," Aunt Bess corrected.

"Yeah, and whoever pays the most money gets to eat."

Mandy couldn't help but smile at his simplified definition. There was much more to it than that.

"It's going to be two weeks from Saturday," Ira said.

"That's just enough time for us to get our boxes decorated," Aunt Bess said, glancing at Mandy.

"You're taking a box?" Ira's voice rose to a squeak.

"I certainly am," Aunt Bess declared. "It's to raise money for the school. A lot of women will bring boxes."

"I wish I had some money," Ira said. "I'd buy yours."

Aunt Bess smiled at him, then turned to Mandy. "We can get some boxes from the store and cover them with wallpaper. And we'll make some paper flowers to put on them."

"I don't know if I'm going to take a box," Mandy said.

"Well, that's up to you," Aunt Bess said through pursed lips. "We'll decorate two just in case. Maybe your mother will take one."

The decorating might be fun, Mandy admitted to herself, especially making the paper flowers. They'd have to be careful though, and not let anyone see the finished boxes. Ira would see them, of course. She wondered if he could keep the secret.

Later at supper, Ira explained everything to his mother. "Aunt Bess says you might take a box," he finished.

"I don't know. I may have to work that day." She paused and looked from Ira to Mandy. Then she drew in a deep breath and said, "I want to tell you all something." All thoughts of the box social were swept away by her serious tone. "I've decided to buy Armstrong's store."

Mandy tried to swallow the aching lump in her throat. She hung her head and squeezed her eyes shut. This had to be a terrible nightmare. But it must be real because her mother was calmly explaining the finances to Aunt Bess.

"The down payment is four thousand dollars. I only have twenty-nine hundred, so I'll have to get a loan from the bank for the rest."

"It seems like a fair deal," Aunt Bess said.

"Yes. There's someone else interested in buying it, but Mr. Armstrong gave me first chance."

First chance! Mandy silently echoed. Mrs. Fulton had given them first chance to buy the Fulton place too. Her mother seemed to have forgotten all about that. But how could she? Until the very day Mandy's father left for the war, they had planned and schemed and dreamed of buying the Fulton place. Now the idea was being brushed aside, like an unwanted cobweb.

"The bank may not want to loan you the money without collateral," Aunt Bess said.

"I found that out. The bank in Garnet Creek wouldn't give it to me, so I'm going to First National. If they won't make the loan, then I guess I'll have to give up the idea."

Mandy ducked her head so the others couldn't see the hope in her eyes. There was still a chance. If her mother couldn't get the bank loan, then they would return to Garnet Creek in August, just as they'd planned. Maybe by that time they'd have enough money saved to buy the Fulton place, and life would come right again . . . almost right again.

The day her mother went to the bank, Mandy could hardly keep her mind on her school work. With a longing that left her almost physically sick, she prayed the bank would refuse to make the loan. Her mother's failure meant her own success.

A few minutes after Mandy and Ira arrived home from school, their mother came through the back door. Recognizing the defeat in her mother's eyes, Mandy listened with mounting elation.

"You were right, Aunt Bess. They wouldn't make the loan without collateral."

Aunt Bess spoke up at once. "You know you could use this farm as collateral."

"Absolutely not! I won't let you risk your home."

Aunt Bess merely nodded and went on kneading the great lump of dough on the floured tabletop.

Mandy's spirits soared, and she began to plan again. They would return to Garnet Creek at the end of summer. In the meantime, all she had to do was get through the rest of the school year. Summer would take care of itself. Mandy wondered if Aunt Bess was making cinnamon rolls. She might be bossy and the very devil to live with, but her cinnamon rolls were a little bit of heaven.

chapter ❧ eleven

On Sunday afternoon, Mandy's mother came from the store, carrying two boxes about the size of peck baskets. "These should hold plenty of food for a picnic," she said to Mandy.

"Are you going to the box social?" Mandy asked.

"No, I can't. I have to work at the store."

"We'll only need one then, 'cause I'm not taking a box."

"It's for your school, Mandy. Don't you think you ought to participate?"

"I don't want to eat with somebody I don't know," Mandy said. Besides, it isn't my school, she silently added. There wasn't much more than a month of school left, and next year she'd be back in her old school. She hoped!

"How's Mr. Armstrong?" she asked. "Has he sold the store?"

"Not yet," her mother said. "He's still hoping that I'll be able to buy it."

"But you can't," Mandy said. "You don't have the money."

"I know that, Mandy," her mother said, frowning. "But he's going to wait a few weeks and see if I can get it. I don't have much hope," she added in a subdued voice.

Mandy could almost feel her mother's longing for the store. Was it because she worried about making a living or was it something else? Suddenly, it came to Mandy that her mother didn't want to live in the Fulton place. In fact, she was doing everything she could to avoid it. Mandy ground her teeth together, feeling betrayed by the one person who should be on her side. Couldn't she see that they needed the Fulton place? Then Mandy thought of something.

"Mama, why don't we write to Mrs. Fulton and tell her we want to buy her place? I'll bet we could make a living off of the apple orchard."

Her mother's quiet words surprised Mandy. "Maybe you're right, Mandy. Let me think about it a while."

Mandy walked on air the next few days. It looked as though things were falling into place at last. She was so happy that when she and Aunt Bess began decorating the boxes, even the box social sounded like fun. Maybe she should take a box.

After mixing some wallpaper paste, they sorted through a box of scraps and chose a yellow wallpaper with orange and brown birds. Once the boxes were covered, they got out yellow crepe paper and began fashioning roses for extra decorations.

Mandy tried, but her hands wouldn't do what her brain told them to do. She squeezed the paper too tightly, crushing it out of shape, and when she tried to curl the petal edges with the scissors, she ripped the paper.

She stopped to watch Aunt Bess's knobby, crooked fingers handling the fragile paper. Were these the same hands that wielded the hammer and chopped off the lambs' tails? It seemed incredible that they were also capable of such fine artistry.

Mandy took up the scissors with renewed determination, but the paper tore again.

"Watch," Aunt Bess said, taking the scissors from her. "Don't pull so hard on the paper. Just use your thumb to stretch it lightly over the blade."

Biting her bottom lip, Mandy kept at it, awkwardly working and shaping, until at last she had enough whole petals to make a flower. Then with Aunt Bess advising and guiding Mandy's fingers with her own, they brought the petals together to form a perfect rose.

Mandy's eyes gleamed. "It's beautiful." Aunt Bess smiled to herself and went back to work.

A while later they were interrupted by a knock at the door. When Aunt Bess stepped outside, Mandy could hear Dean explaining that he'd come to pick out his ewe. Aunt Bess came back into the kitchen and dug around in the cupboard until she found a small jar of yellow paint. Then she turned to Mandy.

"You can come along, Mandy. We'll tend to the sheep while we're out there."

For several days, the expectant ewes had been confined to the lot behind the barn. When they appeared on the verge of lambing, Aunt Bess made a penned space for them inside the barn. Mildred and her twins had been returned to the flock, along with the injured yearling, hobbling on its splinted leg. The rest of the yearlings still went out to the pasture every day, but Mandy seldom had to go after them. They came at her call now, knowing there would be grain waiting.

Mandy followed Aunt Bess and Dean through the gate, closing it behind her. When she turned, she saw the entire flock hurrying toward them, but their eagerness didn't bother her anymore. Without noticing just how or when it had happened, Mandy had lost her fear of them. In fact, it amused her now to think that at one time she had been afraid of such meek and gentle animals.

Aunt Bess scratched the boldest ones behind their ears and waited. She'd promised Dean he could pick the ewe he wanted, and Mandy knew she would not interfere. Though the flock was smaller because of those already with lambs, there were still over twenty, too many for a quick selection. Dean walked among them, lifting a chin, bending to feel an animal's legs, rubbing a hand over its soft, clean wool.

Mandy smiled, watching him. He seemed eager

to select one, and yet he appeared reluctant too, perhaps unwilling to settle on one when there were so many possible choices.

A ewe came to him from the edge of the flock and nuzzled his hand. Finding nothing, she stood beside him and watched the other animals milling about. When Dean bent over and rubbed her ears, she leaned against his leg in a kind of affectionate trust. It seemed to Mandy that instead of Dean choosing a ewe, a ewe had chosen him.

"This one," he said to Aunt Bess.

Aunt Bess nodded and opened her small jar of paint as Dean knelt beside the ewe, an arm draped over her back to hold her still. Using a stick, Aunt Bess daubed a streak of paint along one hind leg.

"I'll have the money for you pretty soon," Dean said.

"How will you get her to your place?" Aunt Bess asked.

"I'm going to see if Andy Moore will pick her up in his truck."

"He'll do it," Aunt Bess said. "He goes by here every afternoon after work."

Still kneeling, Dean took the ewe's head in his hands and spoke to her. "I'm going to call you Molly," he said, then stood up and grinned at Mandy and Aunt Bess. "I always liked the name Molly."

"It's as good as any," Aunt Bess said, turning away.

As Dean and Mandy walked toward the gate,

Dean said, "That was a good idea you had for making money . . . the box social."

"It was June's idea. I've never even been to a box social. It doesn't sound like much fun."

"It is kind of risky for a girl," Dean said, grinning. "She never knows who will get her box." When Mandy made a face, he added, "Course, if she knows who she wants to eat with, she can tell him how it's decorated."

Was Dean hinting that he wanted to buy her box? "Aunt Bess is taking a box," Mandy said, as if she hadn't understood his subtle suggestion.

"I wouldn't mind buying her box. She's a good cook."

How could he afford to buy a box? He was having a hard time just getting the money for the ewe. He'd never spend his sheep money! Mandy asked anyway. "Are you thinking of buying a box?"

"If I had the money, and if I knew I could get the right one," he said, "but a fellow can never really be sure." Until that moment, Mandy had not realized just how uncomfortable a box social might be for a boy too.

Later in the week as Mandy and June came in from afternoon recess, they heard a commotion and noticed a crowd around Mr. Mills's desk. When they got closer, they could see that the green jar was the center of everyone's attention. Mr. Mills picked it up and dumped out all the money, and for several moments the sound of jingling coins filled the silence. Then Mr. Mills spoke.

"There's exactly eight dollars missing," he said. His calm voice carried over the students' angry exclamations. "Please take your seats."

When everyone was seated, Mr. Mills stood before them, his hands clasped in front of him. "This is very serious," he began. "Someone has removed money from the map fund, either as a joke or as an outright theft. If it was meant as a practical joke, will you please return the money to me . . . now."

He paused and looked around the room. There was no movement, no sound, only Mr. Mills's roving gaze that burned like scalding water when it touched a person in passing.

"Will you please empty your desks. Place everything on top where I can see it."

His thorough search took more than an hour. When every book, every lunch sack, every pencil box had been examined, when every pocket had been turned inside out, the money still had not been found.

Mr. Mills stared a long moment at the green jar, then looked over the classroom. "If the person who took the money will come to me after school, I will accept the money along with his or her apology, and no more will be said about it. I remind you again, this is very serious business."

Mandy gripped the edges of her desk, thinking

of Dean. He needed money to pay for the ewe. She knew how much he wanted that sheep, so much that he'd probably do anything to get it. Dean was absent today, but Mr. Mills had searched his desk and found nothing. Anyway, if Dean had stolen the money, Mandy reasoned, he would have taken it with him.

Just then she saw Curtis staring at her, a secretive smile on his face. Maybe he took the money. She'd been so certain that Dean took it, she hadn't considered there might be other thieves in the school. She remembered how enthusiastic Curtis had been about the box social. He could have taken the money to buy a box.

Mandy was confused now. Maybe the thief was neither Dean nor Curtis. She looked around the classroom, wondering who else had the nerve to steal the money. Her breath came out in a sigh. Nobody had as much nerve as Dean.

After school let out, Mandy went down the steps to look for Ira. She found him helping Mrs. Nichols and signalled that she'd wait for him outside. She was reading in her history book when she saw Curtis round the corner of the building. Instead of passing on by, he walked over and stood in front of Mandy.

"I know who took the money," he said. "Everybody knows who it was. Why do you suppose Dean's not here today?"

Mandy couldn't control the sudden flare of anger. "Maybe you're accusing him just to hide the fact that you took it."

"I didn't take it!"

His indignant denial only made Mandy more suspicious. She knew a thief was also a liar. She'd learned that from hard, personal experience. She remembered the day in Garnet Creek when she'd picked up a pink comb from the windowsill in the cloakroom. Later a girl accused her of stealing it and told the teacher. To hide her misdeed, Mandy lied, saying her mother had bought it for her.

She was allowed to keep the comb, but that was not the end of her woes. At home, when her mother asked where she got the comb, she'd lied again and said a girl at school had given it to her. She couldn't enjoy the comb after that, and finally, on the way to school one day, she threw it into the creek. Thieves are always liars, she reminded herself.

Curtis still stood there in front of her, denouncing Dean. "Everyone knows he took it . . . even Mr. Mills."

Mandy knew deep inside that Curtis was probably right, and she hated him for being right. She jumped to her feet, and surprising both herself and Curtis, gave him a shove that sent him reeling. He stumbled over a rock and fell backward on the ground. Without looking at him again, Mandy grabbed her books and ran across the school yard.

She got as far as the fork in the road before she remembered that she'd left Ira behind. She sat down beside the road to wait for him.

She could think of nothing but the stolen money. Why had Dean taken it when he seemed as happy as everyone else about getting a big map? She thought of the ewe. He wanted that animal as badly as she wanted the Fulton place. She could understand that kind of wanting. But this wasn't just another of his insignificant thefts; this was a crime against everyone in the school.

As soon as Mandy and Ira arrived home, Ira dropped his books and took off for the store. Aunt Bess was standing by the kitchen table, slicing apples into a pie crust.

"He's certainly in a hurry," she remarked, then looked more closely at Mandy. "Is something wrong?"

"Someone stole some of our map money," Mandy replied.

"Do they know who took it?"

"No," Mandy said, then blurted out, "but I know. Dean took it."

"Don't be too quick to accuse him," Aunt Bess said.

"You know he's been trying to get money to buy the sheep from you." Mandy stopped as she recalled Dean's remarks about the box social. Maybe even then he was planning his theft. "And he's talking about buying a box at the box social."

"Well, if he stole the money and uses it to buy a box, it will go back in the fund. That's one consolation."

Aunt Bess made it sound almost trivial. Mandy silently hoped it wasn't true, but if Dean bid on a box at the box social, it would be proof enough for her that he took it.

"I have some good news," she heard Aunt Bess saying. "I think I've figured out how your mother can get the rest of the down payment for the store. It just came to me a while ago, so she doesn't even know about it yet."

The moment Aunt Bess's words registered, Mandy's mind rushed to reject them. Good news! It was horrible, unthinkable! She was so stunned she could hardly follow Aunt Bess's explanation.

"I always sell off some of my lambs when they're weaned. The wool money goes for taxes, but the lamb money is just extra." She was busy with her pie and did not notice the distress on Mandy's face. "I think we'll be able to meet Mr. Armstrong's terms," she finished.

Mandy clamped her jaws tight. Aunt Bess talked as though the deal was partly hers. Why did she have to interfere? With her generous offer of help, she was stealing Mandy's father from her, just as surely as Dean had stolen the map money. Mandy was sure that the time would come when she would try to see her father's face and there would be nothing there. Dazed, she went off to her room.

Later, when her disappointment had slackened, she went to call in the yearlings. As she entered the barn, she heard faint bleats coming from the shadowy lambing pens and knew more ewes had delivered. Stopping beside one pen, she stared at the twin lambs huddled against their mother. Her earlier feelings of good will toward the sheep had vanished. Every lamb born now was a hindrance, a living, growing obstacle standing between her and the life she wanted in Garnet Creek.

chapter ✤ twelve

Mandy awoke in the early morning darkness, rousing slowly from a strange dream. She'd been trying to drive a flock of lambs along a country road, but they were skittish and wild and uncontrollable. They ran into the ditches, up the road banks; some even jumped through the barbed wire fences, all desperate to get away. They seemed to be terrified of her.

She sat up and rubbed her eyes. Lambs were so playful and trusting, like small, shy children. She could never hurt any of them. But they were certainly hurting her. They were making it possible for her mother to buy the store.

When Mandy arrived at the breakfast table, she noticed the gleam of excitement in her mother's eyes. She slid into her chair and reached for a slice of toast.

"I guess Aunt Bess told you, Mandy, that she's going to lend us the money she gets from the lambs."

Mandy braced herself to meet her mother's

sparkling gaze. "Yes, she told me." Then her glance slid over to Aunt Bess. She hadn't been able to think of anything else but the lambs since Aunt Bess told her. She hated the idea, even hated the lambs. It was ironic that it was her job to look after them and keep them safe.

"What if they don't bring enough money?" Mandy blurted out.

"Aunt Bess says there will be enough, or almost. Anyway, we can scrape together a little bit. You still have the thirty-five dollars that your . . . that you've been saving, don't you?"

"That money wasn't for a store," Mandy said, flashing an angry glance at her mother.

"If I need to, I'll borrow it, then pay you back later," her mother went on, not even hearing Mandy's bitter protest.

Mandy was not ready to give up yet. "You remember, Mama, when we talked about the Fulton place and the apple orchard? You promised you'd write to Mrs. Fulton."

"I didn't promise to write to her, Mandy. I only promised to think about your suggestion. I have thought about it, and I believe that we can have a more secure life with the store."

It doesn't seem to matter what I want, Mandy thought, pushing her chair away from the table. They were going to buy the store, and there was nothing she could do about it. She thought of her father then, aching for him, knowing that if he'd been there, everything would have been different.

Though the day was sunny, Mandy's mind was filled with gloom as she walked to school. She felt a little better when June came and sat in the seat next to her and talked about the box she was decorating. "It's green and silver," she whispered, looking around to make sure no one had heard. "And I'm going to have fried chicken and corn salad and apple pie. Have you decided, Mandy? Are you bringing a box?"

"I don't know," Mandy said, catching some of June's enthusiasm. "Aunt Bess and I decorated two boxes. We thought Mama might bring one, but she has to work that day."

"Most of the mothers will bring boxes," June said.

"Is your mother bringing one?" Mandy asked.

"No," June said. She hesitated a moment before continuing. "My mother died when I was born." The shock must have shown on Mandy's face because June hurried on. "I guess I never mentioned it before."

Mandy lowered her head. So that's why June talked only of her father and brother. And when she spoke of her apple pie, it really was her apple pie. A depressing guilt settled over Mandy. She'd been so wrapped up in herself, she'd never considered that others might have as great a loss as hers. Mandy thought of June growing up without a mother and consoled herself that at least she'd had her father for a while. She had a sudden desire to tell June about him.

"My father was killed in the war," she said. It was the first time she'd ever spoken those words to anyone but Ira.

June gave a soft moan, then leaned over and laid her arm around Mandy's shoulder. In that quiet moment, they seemed to understand each other as never before. June's silent gesture of sympathy made Mandy change her mind about the box social. It wasn't such a big thing; in fact, it was trivial compared to some things in life. There was no reason why Ira couldn't buy her box. She'd use some of the money her father had sent; her mother was going to take it anyway. She shrugged her shoulders and said, "I guess I'll bring a box."

On the way home that afternoon, Mandy explained to Ira what she wanted him to do at the box social.

"I'll give you the money. You just have to keep bidding until you get it. And don't you dare tell a soul what my box looks like."

"What'll we have to eat?" Ira asked.

"Whatever Aunt Bess puts in her box, I'll have in

mine too," Mandy said. "Are you sure you know what to do?"

"Yeah, it's easy as pie. Hey, are we going to have pie?"

Over the next few days, more and more lambs were born. When Aunt Bess moved a ewe and her lambs back in with the pasturing flock, the emptied pen was immediately occupied by another ewe ready to give birth. Finally, there were only three pregnant ewes left, and one of them was Dean's Molly.

Dean had missed the last four days of school, a thief unable to face his victims, Mandy concluded. She wondered if he would have the nerve to come and pay for the ewe with the stolen money. If Aunt Bess thought the money was stolen, she might refuse payment, might even refuse to sell him the ewe. Mandy kept a special watch on Molly, not really sure whether she did it for Aunt Bess or for Dean.

On the morning of the box social, Mandy woke to a cloudless blue sky. After dressing, she went to Ira's room and nudged him awake. She handed him a five-dollar bill and said, "For goodness sakes, don't lose this. And remember, don't tell anybody which box is mine."

Following a light breakfast, Mandy helped Aunt Bess prepare the picnic lunches. They boiled potatoes for potato salad, then as soon as they were cool enough to handle, Mandy pulled off the thin, wrinkled skins and cut the potatoes into bite-size pieces. The sweet-sour aroma of Aunt Bess's salad dressing made her mouth water.

They fried ham for sandwiches, slices as thick as the bread around it. Mandy took whole sweet pickles, plump and crisp, from a gallon crock and filled two small jelly jars. Last of all, she wrapped cinnamon rolls in waxed paper, two for each box. As she licked the sticky sweetness from her fingers, she could picture Ira's appreciative grin. Once the food was packed inside and the boxes sealed, they wrapped them in blankets so no one would be able to see their decorations when they arrived at school.

A friend of Aunt Bess's, Mrs. Matherson, stopped to get them in her fancy green sedan. Mandy and Ira rode in the spacious back seat, hanging onto the boxes as the bumpy road bounced them into the air.

The only person in the downstairs classroom was Mrs. Nichols, and she smiled and waved a greeting to Mandy and Ira. Quickly, before anyone came in and saw them, they removed the blankets and placed the boxes on the already crowded table. The bright colors, the frills and flowers, the shimmering bows and ribbons, made Mandy catch her breath. Just then, June hurried into the room.

"That's mine," she said, pointing to a square box covered in green crepe paper and tied with silver ribbon. On top was a round white flower made of several layers of lace. "I found that flower in the attic," she added.

"We made our flowers," Mandy said, laying a hand on Aunt Bess's box. She knew it was Aunt Bess's because one of the yellow roses on top had a lavender petal. While they were decorating, they'd decided on that way to mark the boxes so they could tell them apart.

"I'd like to learn how to do that," June said.

"Aunt Bess is teaching me how," Mandy said. "She could teach you too."

"Do you think she would? I could come over anytime she says."

"I'll ask her about it," Mandy said, as they stepped outside.

"I saw Curtis counting his money a while ago," June whispered. "He's got a big roll of bills."

"Where'd he get that much money?" Mandy asked. She and June exchanged a knowing glance, both thinking of the map fund.

"I bet he bids on your box," June said.

"He doesn't know which one is mine, at least I hope he doesn't." A sudden, scary thought flashed through her mind. When Ira bid on her box, Curtis would probably guess it was hers. There had to be some way to sidetrack him. Maybe Ira could bid on Aunt Bess's box too, just long enough to make Curtis think it was Mandy's.

Mandy hurried to find Ira. She'd just explained

what he should do when the big bell began to toll. She dashed inside and pushed her box to the far side of the table so it would be one of the last ones sold. Outside, she slipped into the crowd as people moved closer around the steps. Mr. Mills clapped his hands to get everyone's attention.

"Ladies and gentlemen, thank you for coming. As you know, we're trying to raise money to buy a wall map of the United States. Your participation today will help make that possible. So here's our auctioneer, Mr. Jones."

"That's Curtis's father," June whispered. He was a tall man with fuzzy eyebrows and ruddy cheeks. When Mrs. Nichols handed him a box covered in yellow and black crepe paper, he held it over his head, calling out, "What am I bid for this box of hidden treasure."

"A quarter," came a man's voice from the back of the crowd. Slowly, with mounting enthusiasm, the bids climbed until the box sold for $3.50. After Mr. Mills took the money and recorded it, the auctioneer handed over the box to the happy buyer.

One by one the boxes were brought out and sold. Mandy kept scanning the crowd, wondering if Dean would dare to appear. If he stole the money so he could buy a box, why wasn't he here bidding on one? Now that she thought about it, Curtis seemed the more likely thief. He was there and carrying a lot of money.

When June's green and silver box was offered, June grinned at Mandy and bounced up and down on her toes. There was a rush of bids, but at last only two persons were left. Mandy recognized June's father as one of the bidders. After several minutes of rapid-fire bidding, June's father threw up his hands in good-natured defeat. The crowd laughed when he said, "There goes my apple pie."

The other man moved to the steps and paid six dollars for June's box. As he retreated into the crowd, he looked over at June and winked.

"You know him?" Mandy asked in a hushed voice.

"Yeah, that's my uncle Jim."

The next box displayed was Aunt Bess's, clearly marked by the rose with the lavender petal. If Ira was going to bid, Mandy thought, he'd better get ready. As the auctioneer lifted the box, Mandy heard Ira open with a quarter bid. When the price reached two dollars, he dropped out, but their scheme had worked. Curtis took the bait, raising every bid until finally he bought the box for five dollars. Poor Aunt Bess, Mandy thought.

When Mandy's box was brought out, she dropped her head and edged backward into the crowd. The auctioneer informed everyone that there were only three boxes left, and so bidding was brisk from the start.

Mandy listened for Ira's voice, but there were only men bidding. Where was he? As the bidding continued without him, Mandy fought down a mounting panic. Why did she ever let herself get into this predicament!?

"Three dollars and fifty cents," came a familiar voice, not Ira's, but one she recognized. Dean was bidding on her box. A man just behind Mandy offered four dollars. A lump rose in her throat that she couldn't seem to swallow down. If Ira wasn't going to buy her box, she hoped and prayed Dean would buy it. The eight dollars he'd taken from the map fund should be more than enough.

Mandy stood there in the crowd, head bowed, her eyes shut tight. Suddenly, she realized that Dean wasn't bidding anymore. She sucked in her breath and held it. Two men were still bidding on her box, $5.50, $6.00, $6.50. The bidding stopped at $7.00. When the auctioneer finally called "Sold," a short, gray-haired man with a silvery beard came out of the crowd to pay for his purchase. At that moment, Mandy wished she'd never heard of a box social.

Moments after the last box was sold, the crowd splintered apart. Amid the backslapping, joking, and friendly greetings, the school yard bloomed with bright blankets and colorful boxes. Hotdogs and lemonade and wedges of pie were already being sold in Mrs. Nichols's classroom to those without box dinners.

Mandy saw Aunt Bess walk over to Curtis, place

her hand on the box he was holding and say something to him. He was unable to hide his dismay. His eyes sought out Mandy, dazed, disbelieving. She knew how he felt, but she didn't waste any sympathy on him. She had her own ordeal to face.

Before she could locate the little, bearded man who'd bought her box, June came running up. "Come on. We'll sit together."

"I have to find . . ." Mandy started, but June was pulling her toward a group of men spreading a red plaid blanket in the grass. The bearded man was one of them.

June skipped ahead, then turned to wait for Mandy. "I want you all to meet my friend, Mandy," she said. "Mandy, you know my father, and this is my brother, Danny, and my uncle Jim."

Mandy nodded to each of them in turn, then couldn't stop her gaze from flitting to the unnamed man who stood there holding her box.

June grinned at her. "And this is my Grandpa Calley."

Mandy's shoulders drooped in relief. Being June's grandfather made him almost a friend. June must have told him which box was hers, Mandy decided. Maybe she'd been planning it ever since that day they'd talked about the parents they had lost.

Mandy tried to participate in the easy conversation, but she couldn't keep from looking around for Ira and Dean. They both had a lot of explaining to do. In spite of what had and had not happened, Mandy began to relax. She'd learned one thing today. It didn't take years to make a friend, if that person was someone like June.

chapter ✤ thirteen

As lunches were finished and lunch boxes packed away, people began drifting toward the ball field behind the schoolhouse. It lay at the bottom of a steep, grassy hill that provided ideal seats for spectators.

Mandy and June took a seat overlooking third base and watched as two teams were organized from the pool of hopeful players. This was a community game, June explained, where anyone, no matter what his or her age or skill, would have the opportunity to play.

Mandy could see what June meant. The teams were made up of an odd assortment of big and little people. June's brother, Danny, stood far out in center field, and a plump, sixth-grade girl was getting ready to pitch. Mandy stared when she saw Ira on first base, pounding his fist into an oversized glove. There he was, acting as if nothing out of the ordinary had happened. Just wait until this is over, Mandy silently promised.

It was a close rivalry, with the score tied at twelve

in the seventh inning. As the game progressed, the afternoon sun warmed both the players and the hillside fans. During the eighth inning, Mandy and June went down to the pump to get a drink of water. June worked the handle up and down and Mandy drank from her cupped hands. Then they changed places. Mandy froze when she saw Dean striding toward her.

"I'd like to talk to you," he said in a gruff voice.

June's gaze flitted from one to the other. "I'll go on back," she said to Mandy and walked off.

Dean cupped his hands under the metal spout and Mandy pumped them full. Once he'd finished drinking, he wiped his hands dry on his trousers and gazed across the valley toward Aunt Bess's farm. Finally, he turned to Mandy, a crooked smile on his face. "I tried," he said.

Mandy stared at him for a moment, then she too gazed across at the greening hill rising behind Aunt Bess's barn. The sheep were up there, she could see them moving. Her gaze swung back to Dean.

"What happened?" was all she asked, but the query held a dozen questions. Why haven't you been to school? Why did you take the money? Why did you bid on my box? Why didn't you buy it? Why do you have to steal?

"I wanted to buy your box. I planned to buy it." He stopped and inhaled a long breath.

Mandy's voice was blunt, cold. "What were you going to use for money?"

Dean looked at her, biting his lip. He bent over and picked up a stone, then turned and hurled it clear across the road. "I wanted to buy your box," he said again.

He still wouldn't come right out and admit he'd taken the money. He'd stolen it so that he could buy her box, and it made Mandy feel like an accomplice in the theft. She studied him, the stiff set of his shoulders, arms folded tight, one foot kicking at a clump of grass. She guessed that if she was going to get any answers, she'd have to ask some hard questions.

"Did you take the map money?" she asked.

Dean picked up a small, gray stone and rubbed it clean of dirt. For several moments he tossed the stone from one hand to the other. When he finally looked at Mandy, his gaze wavered and fell away. "One day after school, while Mr. Mills was downstairs talking to Mrs. Nichols, I went up the fire escape and got it."

The feelings that overwhelmed Mandy then were raw and jumbled. She'd wanted answers, and she'd finally got one, one that hurt.

"But if you had the money and planned to buy my box, why didn't you?"

Dean turned to face her, his gaze steady now.

"That's just it. I don't have the money. It's gone."

"Gone! But you bid on my . . ."

Dean interrupted her with a wave of his hand. "I figured Ira would be buying your box, so I talked him into letting me bid on it in his place. Course, I didn't have any money, so he gave me the five . . ."

"You mean you were going to buy my box . . . with *my* money!" Mandy's eyes widened with disbelief. When Dean gave her a lopsided grin, she heaved a sigh of exasperation. If the whole affair weren't so mixed up, it would be almost laughable. She shook her head, trying to make sense out of what Dean had just told her. He'd taken the map money so he could buy her box, but for some reason, he didn't have it anymore. Now she was angry and wanted the whole truth. "Where *is* the map money?" she demanded.

"It's a long story," Dean said. He took a deep breath before he went on. "I was going to get ten dollars for digging a ditch for Mr. Blakely. When he paid me, I planned to put the eight dollars back in the jar."

Mandy waited. He still hadn't explained what happened to the money.

"My dad took all my money. He even took the money I'd saved to buy the ewe. He used it to buy a radio. A radio!" he repeated, as if he didn't expect Mandy to believe it, as if he didn't believe it himself. "And what was left, he spent on whiskey." There was a hoarseness in his voice as he muttered, "Damn him."

Mandy could feel how much he'd been hurt, and for a few seconds, she almost hated Dean's father. But then she saw the cruel justice of it. Dean's father had merely stolen the money that Dean had stolen first. She was angry at both of them, and accusing words came tumbling out.

"That day at the store, when you helped my mother pick up the money she'd dropped, you kept a quarter, didn't you?"

The look on Dean's face was answer enough. "I thought so," Mandy said, her eyes level and unrelenting.

"I'll return the quarter as soon as I make some money," Dean said. "But it may be a while. I saw Mr. Blakely yesterday, and he told me he didn't need me after all."

That settled everything, Mandy thought. He couldn't buy the ewe, and he couldn't return the stolen money. His makeshift scheme of theft and repayment had fallen apart.

"Would you tell your Aunt Bess I won't be getting the ewe," Dean said.

The hopelessness in his voice sent Mandy's own spirits plunging. She just couldn't be angry at him for trying to make a dream come true.

"Yes," she said, picturing the friendly ewe that had chosen Dean that day in the barnyard. "Molly hasn't lambed yet," she told him.

Dean looked down at the stone in his hand, then

carelessly tossed it away. "It doesn't make any difference now."

Moments later, there was a swelling noise from the ball field, then people came streaming across the school yard like ants over an ant hill. The ball game was over.

Dean shoved his hands into his pockets and with one final glance at Mandy, walked away. He headed for the road, head lowered, his shoulders hunched like a tired, old man. Mandy shared his sadness. After all, he was losing the one thing in the world he wanted. She knew how that felt.

June appeared at Mandy's side, and she too stared after Dean. "What's wrong?" she asked. When Mandy explained everything, June nodded, as if she'd expected as much.

"He doesn't have any hope of getting a sheep any time soon," Mandy said. "He may just give up even trying."

"Dad says if you want something real bad, you just have to grab ahold and hang on, like a robin with a getaway worm," June said.

It sounded like good advice, though Mandy knew that sometimes it still didn't work. She wanted to live at the Fulton place, but her mother and Aunt Bess had conspired to keep her here in Parrish Grove. And there didn't seem to be a thing she could do about it.

On the ride back to the farm, Mandy scolded Ira

for abandoning her at the box social. "I thought I could trust you," she said.

"I figured you'd rather have Dean buy your box than me. Besides, Tappy bought his mother's box, and he said I could eat with them."

"So you gave Dean my money to buy my box!" Mandy exclaimed. "By the way, where is my money?"

Ira reached in his pocket and pulled out the crinkled bill. "You ought to be glad Curtis didn't buy your box."

Mandy just glared at him, then gazed out the car window to hide her smile. She wouldn't admit it to Ira, but the box social had turned out surprisingly well, considering all the bad things that could have happened.

At supper Mandy listened with halfhearted interest as Aunt Bess told about sharing her box dinner with Curtis. "He's the one who was picking on you, wasn't he?" she asked Ira. When Ira nodded, she went on. "Well, I told him there'd be no more of that." She ignored Ira's wide grin. "By the time we got to the cinnamon rolls, we understood each other."

Though Mandy had told Aunt Bess she thought Dean stole the map money, she decided not to tell about his confession. She just explained that Dean's father had taken all his money and bought a radio. "Now he's not going to be able to get Molly," she finished.

"Well, he'll get her sometime, I'm sure," Aunt

Bess said. "I never saw a boy want anything the way he wants that sheep."

If Aunt Bess understood Dean's great ambition to own a flock of sheep, she should be willing to help him, Mandy thought to herself. Why didn't she just give him the ewe now and let him pay for it when he got the money? Aunt Bess answered the unspoken question.

"I could let him take the ewe now and pay me later, but he might as well learn that things don't come easy."

After what his father had done, Dean must know that already, Mandy mused. He would start saving money again for the ewe, but he'd have to pay back what he'd stolen first. She understood how discouraged he must be. It's hard to hold on to a dream, she thought, when nobody believes in it but you.

She remembered the money in her dresser drawer. She had thirty-five dollars again, since Ira had returned the unused five-dollar bill. There was more than enough to buy Molly. But she couldn't give up the money. Her father had sent it for only one purpose, to help them get the Fulton place. Though that seemed all but impossible now, Mandy couldn't even consider using the money for anything else.

chapter ❧ fourteen

A storm came up that night after dark. Great streaks of lightning ripped across the black sky and thunder rattled the window panes. Mandy went to the barn with Aunt Bess to see about the sheep. Making the rounds of the lambing pens, they found that Molly had given birth to twins. It must have happened earlier in the evening because the lambs already moved with confidence on their knobby, crooked legs.

"I think we'll move the sheep to the lower pasture where the grass is better," Aunt Bess said. Mandy nodded, only half listening. "And later this week, we'll dock some of the week-old lambs."

That got Mandy's attention, and she almost groaned out loud. She'd hoped maybe Aunt Bess would do that job some day while she was at school.

The sheep appeared confused the next morning when Mandy and Aunt Bess herded them through the gate into the new pasture. They milled around the fence, bleating, uncertain, skeptical of the change in routine. Gradually hunger overcame their caution, and they strung out along the muddy stream, nibbling at the tender new grass.

It was still early in the evening when Mandy went after the sheep. Another storm was building up in the hills and thunder rolled down the valley announcing its approach. She didn't want the sheep to get caught out in the pasture in a storm like the one they'd had last night.

Striding along the stream that drained the low pasture, she was soon perspiring in the unseasonably warm air. She must have walked a half mile or more before she spied the sheep. Drawing nearer, she could see the flock knee-deep in grass. They'd crossed the stream to the island she'd seen from the top of the hill a few days earlier. Despite last night's rain, the stream was still only a few inches deep in most places. It posed no obstacle for the sheep.

Mandy cupped her hands to her mouth and called them. The ewes and yearlings started for the stream, and by the time they had waded across, the lambs were close behind, splashing through the water without fear. It's a good thing the sheep follow each other, Mandy thought. Those frisky lambs might get in trouble on their own.

Excitement was building at school over the wall map. The box social had proved successful, raising $93.00, giving them a grand total of $111.36 in the map fund. They were not far from the needed amount of $128.00.

One day, Mr. Mills announced that the stolen money had been returned to the fund. There was a rising chorus of comments and questions.

"Who took it?" Curtis called out. "I'll bet I . . ."

"The money is back and the matter is closed," Mr. Mills said. "Now I suggest you eighth graders get busy on your arithmetic."

Mandy couldn't help but sneak a glance at Dean, wondering where he'd gotten the eight dollars. He'd been to school every day since the box social, but he hardly talked to anyone, including Mandy. She didn't have to talk to him to feel the sadness about him, the air of something lost.

At recess, Mandy and June decided to clean out their desks. They talked back and forth as they worked.

"I told Aunt Bess that you wanted to learn how to make paper flowers. She said you could come anytime. How about Saturday?"

"Sure," June said, grinning. "I'll be there bright and early. It's only a mile walk."

Just then, Dean appeared beside Mandy's desk. "Cleaning house?" he asked with a flash of his former good humor.

"Yes. You ought to try it," she countered. She was glad he was finally talking.

"How's Molly?" he asked, his eyes dropping away from her watchful gaze.

"She's fine. She had twins over the weekend."

Dean turned his head and stared out the window for several moments. "I guess your Aunt Bess will be selling most of the lambs once they're weaned. There's a fellow over in the next county always buys her extras."

"Yes, she's going to sell them," Mandy replied, trying not to think about the transaction and what it meant.

When June went off to speak to Mr. Mills, Dean leaned forward and rested his arms on Mandy's desk. His words were quiet, meant only for her. "I talked to Mr. Mills about the map money," he said. "He put the eight dollars back in the fund, and I'm to repay him when I get it." Then he stared out the window again, a frown darkening his face.

Was he hating his father or hating himself for everything that had gone wrong? Mandy wondered. At least he had a chance to set some of it right again. His troubled gaze swung back to Mandy.

"Mr. Mills said I owed a debt to the school, aside from the money. He told me to decide how I wanted to pay it."

Mr. Mills was right, Mandy thought. Dean had betrayed everyone and he deserved some kind of punishment.

"I thought about it for a couple of days," Dean went on. "Then I decided I'd stay an hour after school every day. I told Mr. Mills I'd straighten up, clean the blackboards, and sweep. He agreed to it."

"You won't have much time left for making money," Mandy said.

"I'll have Saturdays," Dean replied. Suddenly, his face brightened and he reached out and gave Mandy's braid a tug. His smile revealed the ghost of his old, easy self.

"I still wish I'd had the eight dollars to buy your box," he said. Then he turned and strolled down the aisle, leaving Mandy shaking her head and wondering whether he was truly sorry for all his thefts.

In the days that followed, storms pounded the valley. The low land between Aunt Bess's farm and the school lay under a shallow, spreading lake. Each day the flood deepened.

One morning Mandy and Ira found the county road awash, shutting off their route to the schoolhouse. Along with several other children who took that road to school, they waited to see if the school bus would drive through it. The bus driver, understanding their problem, stopped and motioned them aboard. They had to stand up because all of the seats were full, but at least they were high and dry. Despite water washing over the bottom step, the bus had no trouble getting through. Mandy and Ira came home the same way, standing in the bus's crowded aisle, watching the big vehicle plow a furrow through the swirling water.

The rising waters and endless storms were on everyone's mind. Not only were croplands and pastures under water, but many roads had become impassable, with no sign of the rains letting up. Aunt Bess talked to Mandy about the sheep, as each day more low-lying pasture disappeared under the flood.

"We'll have to move them back on the hill if the water continues to rise."

"Can sheep swim?" Mandy asked, recalling how the gawky lambs splashed through the stream after their mothers.

"Most animals can swim when they have to," Aunt Bess said, "but sheep get so frightened sometimes that they just can't do anything to help themselves."

For a moment, Mandy thought kindly of the meek animals, then her mind turned cold and hard. Why should she even worry about them? If there were no lambs, she'd be going back to Garnet Creek in the fall.

After school on Friday, Mandy and Ira went to the store to help their mother. Low-hanging clouds warned of yet another storm. The road was still passable, although water crept ever closer to the pavement. On the store steps, they paused to gaze across the road and railroad at the distant brown sea. The creek had crawled out of its meandering channel and blanketed most of the bottomland fields. If the rain doesn't stop soon, Mandy thought, we'll all be heading for high ground, along with Aunt Bess's sheep.

Ira saw his friend, Tappy, coming down the road and ran to meet him, while Mandy entered the store. There were no customers inside, and the dim interior seemed as still as an empty church. She found her mother bent over the counter, scribbling numbers on a pad. There were lines on her face Mandy hadn't noticed before.

"What's wrong, Mama?"

"There are an awful lot of people who owe the store money," she said. "I hope I'm doing the right thing, trying to buy it."

It was the first uncertainty Mandy had heard from her mother about the store purchase. Maybe she didn't really want to buy it anymore. Maybe she'd give it up and return to Garnet Creek.

Mandy took a deep breath. "Wouldn't it be better to go back to Garnet Creek, where everybody knows us?" she asked. Her mother lifted her head, then laid down her pencil and folded her arms across her chest.

"I'm sick and tired of hearing your talk about Garnet Creek, Mandy."

"But Mama . . ." Mandy began, then stopped, realizing they were about to argue again. "I wish Dad was here," she murmured.

Suddenly, her mother leaned across the counter, her eyes glittering with a fiery light. "Don't you bring him into this. He's not here. He has nothing to do with our life now."

Mandy shrank away from the fierce anger, startled, afraid. At last she stretched out a trembling hand. "Don't say that, Mama . . ."

Unheeding, her mother lashed out again. "A real father is someone who's here when you need him. And your father is not here."

"Mama . . . he's still my father, even if he is . . . is . . ." Mandy stopped, unable to say the word. "He's my father . . ." she pleaded. Her mother's next words stung like a slap in the face.

"He's no one's father anymore."

"Mama, how can you . . . don't you still love him?"

"Love him!" her mother burst out, her eyes flashing. "He lied to me. He said he would come back but he didn't."

Mandy remembered her own similar thoughts, and realized how unfair they were. "He wanted to come back, Mama, but he couldn't."

"Why did he go off and enlist without even discussing it with me? He might never have been drafted." She brushed a hand across her forehead. "I hate war, and I hate him for going away and leaving us like this . . . all alone."

Mandy backed away from this woman who looked like her mother but who was really a stranger saying awful things about her father, things she couldn't stand to hear. She turned and darted to the front door. As she snatched it open and rushed out, she collided with Stella coming up the steps. "I'm sorry, Mandy," the woman said, then stopped and reached for Mandy's arm. "What's wrong?"

Mandy jerked away from her and ran down the steps. She rounded the corner of the building into the blowing rain. Somewhere behind her, like voices in a dream, she seemed to hear both Stella and her mother calling her name. But she raced on, blind with tears. By the time she reached Aunt Bess's lane, a stitch in her side forced her to a halt. Bent forward, hands on her knees, she gulped in air and waited for the ache to go away.

The physical pain slowly subsided, but the mental pain of her mother's words bounced around in her brain like a hard rubber ball, ricocheting, rebounding, hurting. Not in a million years would she have thought her mother could say such things. The word *hate* was still ringing in her ears. How could her mother use that word toward her father? Mandy was sure that he had gone to war willingly, but she was also certain that it hurt him to leave them alone. Surely her mother knew that.

Little by little the pain melted down into an iron-hard knot of anger. No matter what her mother did, Mandy would remember her father. She loved him, and though he wasn't there to love her back, she'd do whatever was necessary to keep him close.

chapter ✤ fifteen

Rain came down the valley in slanting sheets of water. The heavy drops drummed on Mandy's head and shoulders, but she made no attempt to hurry. It didn't matter that she was soaked to the skin. The storm around her was nothing compared to the storm inside of her. She couldn't feel anything, couldn't think of anything but her mother's shocking words.

Rather than have to face Aunt Bess's prying questions, Mandy dashed past the house and straight into the barn. Once inside, she sagged down into a pile of musty hay and closed her eyes. If only . . . if only . . . but it didn't do any good to wish for what she could never have. He was gone and he'd never return. Tears spilled over as she vowed once again, "I'll never forget you, Dad."

She sat up and brushed away the tears. When you love someone, you can't forget them. That's what love is, she silently declared. It's remembering; it's being together if only in your memory. She wanted to remember her father's love, but maybe even more important, she wanted to remember her love for him. Loving him made her happy. Loving him was like dancing in sunshine.

It was some time before she became aware of her own discomfort. She swiped at her face and arms and tried to wring the water from her braid. Her wet clothes clung to her like an extra skin.

As she was about to lie back again, she felt the strange stillness around her. Then she remembered. All the ewes, along with their lambs, had been turned out in the pasture. The dull roar of rain on the tin roof prodded Mandy to her feet. The sheep were out there in the hammering storm. She'd better get them into the barn before it got any worse.

She stepped out into the downpour and headed for the pasture. Dark clouds had blacked out the sun, bringing on an early, rainy night. Mandy could see only a few feet around her. How could she ever find the sheep in this darkness? She wondered why they hadn't returned to the barn when the storm hit, but then reminded herself that they were just dumb animals. They didn't understand about weather.

The pasture stream had long since been submerged beneath the flood, but the lay of the land was familiar. Mandy skirted the floodwater, peering into the night. As she wiped water from her eyes, she almost fell over a sheep that suddenly appeared out of the gloom. She grabbed for the wet, woolly body and knelt down, shouting above the thunder. "Where are the others?" If only the animal could tell her.

As she stood up, several more sheep materialized beside her. Maybe they're all here, she thought, and called into the wind. "Whoooee." She waited but no more came.

The sheep gathered close around her, strangely silent. Mandy counted four yearlings and one ewe with twins, and calculated that there were more than a hundred sheep still out there.

She started forward, but when the sheep began following her, she stopped. "Go on back to the barn," she shouted, waving a hand down the valley. Then she groaned aloud. Sheep weren't like people; you couldn't just command them to go somewhere. They had to be led. She'd have to take these back to the barn before she could go after the others.

In the flashes of lightning streaking down from the clouds, Mandy stumbled toward the barn. The sheep remained so close that she kept bumping against them, but when they recognized the barnyard gate, they left her behind.

Mandy paused when a glow appeared just inside

the open barn door. It was Aunt Bess holding a lantern over her head, trying to see through the curtain of rain running off of the barn roof. Mandy ran towards the light.

"Thank goodness you're back," Aunt Bess said.

"Most of the sheep are still out there," Mandy told her, rubbing water out of her eyes. "But I'll find them . . ."

"No!" Aunt Bess commanded. "You're not going out there again. There's too much lightning."

"But they can't stay out in this all night," Mandy said and waved a hand at the open door. "Besides, some of them might be hurt."

"There's nothing we can do until this rain lets up," Aunt Bess said. "They'll find some high ground."

"I'm going after them," Mandy declared, and started for the door. Before Aunt Bess could stop her, she had slipped out into the torrent. Just outside the stream of runoff from the roof, she paused and looked back. She could barely make out Aunt Bess's blurred, watery face, her pleading eyes. "I'll be back in a little while," Mandy called, then turned and took off running.

She strained to see as she ran through pools of standing water on her way back up the valley. Her foot caught on a clump of grass, and she stumbled and fell forward on her hands and knees. She wasn't hurt and she certainly wasn't any wetter. Her braid already felt like an iron chain down her back.

Rising to her feet, she proceeded more carefully, even putting her hands out in from of her when lightning exploded and was gone, leaving her momentarily blinded. She'd never seen such a storm before. Sometimes during a gentle, summer rain she and Ira would go out and play in the puddles, damming up tiny streams and watching them overflow. It was fun, especially on a hot day. This storm was no fun at all. In fact, Mandy felt a dull fear gnawing at her, fear not only for the sheep but for herself too.

Sometimes people got struck by lightning and sometimes people drowned. She'd better hurry and find the rest of the sheep. The only safe place on a night like this was the barn. They were somewhere up ahead of her, she knew that. Surely she could find a hundred sheep.

The lightning came more frequently now, and thunder boomed overhead in sudden, deafening blasts. In a split-second flare of light, she thought she saw something ahead. She moved forward, but before she knew it, she had waded into knee-deep water. She stopped and waited for the light. A brief flash illuminated a river of water rushing around her, swift and muddy. She edged backward until she reached solid ground.

She stared across what must be the main channel of the flood. The sheep couldn't be out there. Nevertheless, she cupped her hands to her mouth and called anyway. "Whoooee." From out of the darkness somewhere in front of her came a faint sound. She recognized it at once. It was a lamb bawling for its mother.

In the next flash, Mandy saw them. It was only a glimpse, but it was enough. The sheep were trapped on the pasture island where she'd found them several days before. The other time when she'd called them, they'd simply forded the shallow stream. Now the floodwater had created a lake around the island, too deep and too wide for them to cross. They were safe for the moment, but Mandy knew that inch by inch the island was losing ground to the rising flood.

Standing there in the driving rain, she tried to figure out how to get the sheep over to the higher pasture. Runoff from the upper valley fed the ever-deepening flood. The grown sheep might be able to swim across it, but the lambs would be swept away. The lambs . . . Mandy's thoughts spun around and around, centering down on those frail, fragile creatures. The lambs! She stared into the darkness in the direction of the island. She couldn't see them but she knew they were there, all but two of Aunt Bess's precious crop of lambs. The lambs that were so important to them all . . .

The ugly idea nibbled at the edge of her mind like a fish nibbling at a baited hook. She couldn't acknowledge it; it was too awful. But a churning anger clawed its way from deep inside of her, quietly at first, then mounting until she shuddered with the storm of it. The idea too ugly to look at moments earlier now crawled into the light. Why not? The lambs were all that stood in her way. They were what made it possible for her mother to buy the store. They were what kept her from her dream.

All she had to do was walk away and let them drown. She could tell Aunt Bess the sheep were stranded, and she couldn't get to them. In a way, it was the truth. Maybe she could get to them right now, but if she hesitated for very long, she'd never reach them.

Mandy turned her back on the flood and jammed her hands into her overall pockets, hunching her shoulders against the rain. She thought of the Fulton place, but when she tried to picture it, the image eluded her. All she could see was the stormy, black world around her. She was trapped in the turmoil of her own mind, knowing what she must do, trying to hold on to the anger that would help her do it.

In the next flash of lightning, she spun around and stared across the floodwater. There was no time to see anything, not even the island itself, but she knew what was out there. The sheep, grown animals and lambs, waited for rescue, helpless and afraid.

Mandy folded her arms tight across her chest

and bowed her head. Rain streamed down inside her collar, into her eyes, down her cheeks. She stuck out her tongue and licked the water from her lips. It was the sharp, stinging taste of salt that made her realize she was crying. Last week she'd resolved to do whatever was necessary to keep her dream, but she'd never imagined anything like this. She couldn't do it! She couldn't let them drown.

Mandy looked in the direction of the island and felt sick to her stomach. How could she save them? Faintly from across the water came the bleats of the trapped animals. Their cries prodded her to action. Maybe when she got to them, she'd know what to do.

She sat down and pulled off her shoes and socks, then with cautious, feeling steps, she waded into the swirling water. It rose at each step, to her knees, her thighs. If only there was some light! When she stepped into a low spot and the water rose above her waist, she leaned against the current to keep from losing her balance. In another two steps, the ground began to slope upward. Moments later, she waded through shallow water and onto bare ground. A long breath whistled out of her lungs.

The sheep crowded around her in the darkness, jostling her, sniffing her clothes. Mandy felt a moment of panic. They were dependent on her; she was their last hope. What if she couldn't save them? Angry, she swiped the water from her eyes. She didn't have time for such thoughts.

Without stopping to consider the enormity of the task ahead of her, she bent and picked up a lamb. Then she stepped back into the flood. As she sank lower in the water, she lifted the lamb higher and higher until she was holding it in front of her face. Thank goodness it didn't squirm or try to get free. The current pulled at her, and she did dancing steps underwater to keep herself upright. When she waded out of the water and set the lamb on firm ground, it gave a weak, pitiful cry for its mother.

Mandy did not hesitate but turned and headed back for the island. The rain had not diminished; in fact, it seemed to be increasing. Raindrops struck the water in a relentless, splattering rhythm. The second trip took more time than the first, but she was determined not to let the storm win. She would save the lambs first, then worry about the grown sheep.

Moments after entering the water for her third trip, a log washed against Mandy's leg. As she pushed it aside, she felt the powerful current catch it and carry it away. Moving on, she suddenly went in over her head. She pushed to the surface and spat out a mouthful of the muddy water, dog-paddling to stay afloat. She must have stepped into the submerged stream bed. The water was too deep now to carry any more lambs over, she knew that, but it was easier to go on than try to go back. Besides, she couldn't abandon the others, not after what she'd almost done.

When she waded up onto the island, some of the sheep were waiting at the water's edge. She sat down among them and hugged her knees close against her chin, shivering from the night chill and her own icy fear. Aunt Bess would be sick with worry. Mandy wondered what her mother would do when she came home and learned that Mandy was out in the storm.

A shudder shook Mandy as she thought of what lay ahead. When the island became completely flooded, when she was certain there was no chance of saving the sheep, she'd swim for the far shore. If she could keep her bearings, she might make it. The grown sheep probably couldn't cross that current, and certainly not the lambs. Mandy felt the weight of the night on her like a soggy blanket. She couldn't lose the lambs!

chapter ✤ sixteen

*T*he sheep were thick around Mandy and every time she moved, they stirred too. She had the odd sensation that they were adrift in a black, endless sea. She wished the clouds would pass on. There might be a light in one of the farm houses across the valley. Any kind of light, even a distant one, would be a comfort on such a night. But the dark was impenetrable. It was like trying to see through a solid, brick wall.

Mandy couldn't be sure how much time had passed, but she knew when the storm finally began to lose its fierceness. The thunder came from a greater distance, and the rain dwindled to a gentle patter. Lightning still lit the sky, but it shone dimly through the clouds, like lamplight through a curtain.

Mandy rose to her feet and moved among the restless sheep, patting one on the back, stroking another's nose. As she paused to stare up at the sky she could not see, a sheep came near and nosed her hand. Mandy knelt and wrapped an arm around the woolly animal, pulling it against her. The sheep didn't try to escape her hard embrace, and Mandy rubbed its ears in thanks. One stiff, matted ear had a notch in it.

"Mildred!" she almost shouted. "What are you doing here? Why didn't you go back to the barn?"

The ewe reached down for a bite of grass, then raised her head again, moving her jaws up and down in a slow, undulating rhythm.

"And where are your babies?" Mandy continued. Mildred's commonplace act of grazing seemed to calm Mandy and give her hope. There was something reassuring too about the sound of her own voice in the darkness. The ewe couldn't talk back, but she'd recognized Mandy, and because they shared the same dire predicament, things didn't seem quite so hopeless.

Mandy felt the floodwater swirl around her feet. It was still rising. She pulled Mildred to higher ground. So far, the sheep had managed to avoid the water by huddling closer and closer together, but Mandy knew it was only a matter of time until there would be no more room to retreat.

She thought of Aunt Bess waiting for her return. If I hadn't been so stubborn, I could be there with her in the warm, dry barn, Mandy thought. But then the sheep would have been all alone.

Someone was bound to come looking for her, if

not tonight, then surely at daylight. She knew one thing for sure: she wasn't leaving this island without the sheep.

Mandy lost all track of time as she sat with an arm over Mildred's back. Suddenly, she drew in her breath and held it, listening. A thin, muffled sound floated through the night, weak and far away. She turned her head one direction, then another, straining to hear. It came again, a distant, muted call, with another close after it.

"Man . . . dee . . ."

"Man . . . dee . . ."

That last call was Ira, Mandy could tell. She jumped up and cupped her hands around her mouth, then swallowed hard and shouted. "Here . . . I'm over here." Again, she heard her name, nearer this time. "Here I am," she shouted. It seemed that hours passed before another call came.

"Man . . . dee . . . where are you?"

Her mother's voice had a wildness in it that Mandy had never heard before. A lump rose in her own throat and, for a moment, she couldn't utter a sound. A deep, deliberate breath helped. "I'm here . . . across the water."

"Are you all right?"

"Yes. I'm over here with the sheep."

"Mandy, can you wade across to us?" her mother called.

Mandy felt the sheep moving around her. They'd heard the voices and crowded down to the water's edge. One ewe bawled into the night, a mournful sound that seemed to be an expression of Mandy's own terrible longing. She had the urge to throw herself into the water and swim to that other shore. It was what they wanted her to do. They wouldn't blame her for leaving the sheep. But she couldn't go. She'd made her decision earlier, and that decision still seemed right.

"The water's too deep, Mama, and it's still rising." It was quiet for so long that Mandy began to wonder if they'd gone away. Then she heard voices carrying clearly across the water, sharp, arguing voices.

"No . . . you can't!"

That was Aunt Bess. Mandy recognized her bossy tone. Moments later a light appeared and it was coming towards Mandy. Its glow bounced off the water, creating two moving lights. Mandy thought she could make out a shadowed face beside the lantern. Tears flooded her eyes. Not only was someone coming to her, but they were bringing a light.

As the wavering light drew nearer, Mandy remembered she should warn them about the drop-off into the stream. Before she could call out, the lantern flew into the air. It came down with a splash, still lit, bobbing on the water. It floated there for a moment, then the current caught it and it disappeared into the night. Mandy stared after it, hardly able to breathe. Then her mother's voice came to her, nearer this time. "Mandy, where are you?"

Mandy stepped forward into the water. "I'm here, Mama."

"Keep talking, Mandy, so I can find you."

"This way . . . you stepped into the stream bed, just like I did. It's not far from there . . ." She stopped, feeling a sudden thrill as the familiar form materialized in front of her. She breathed a sigh and stepped into her mother's open arms.

She stood there, holding on to her mother, filled with a marvelous peace. It was as if the sun had come out and banished the darkness. The night had lost its angry power.

Finally her mother released her. "Aunt Bess came and got me after you left the barn. She and Ira are both over there." She turned and called over the channel she'd just crossed. "I made it, Aunt Bess. I'm all right and Mandy's all right too." Then she turned back to Mandy. "What are you doing over here?"

"The sheep were stranded. I carried two lambs across, then the water got too deep."

"We found the lambs, and your shoes too. How much land is still above water?"

"I haven't been all over the island, but I know it's getting smaller by the minute," Mandy said.

"Well, we'll be able to get back across," her mother

said. "I lost the lantern, but Aunt Bess can guide us over." She bent to push one of the sheep out of her way, her white blouse a moving cloud in the dark.

"I'm not going," Mandy said.

"Oh, don't worry, Mandy. I'll be right alongside you."

"It's not that," Mandy said. "It's the sheep. I'm not leaving them."

"Mandy, you can't stay here!"

Mandy leaned closer to try to see her mother's face. "I can't go," she said.

"Mandy, you are going!" That tone only made Mandy's determination stronger. She would just have to make her mother understand why she couldn't go away and leave them.

"Mama, when I knew the sheep were stranded on this island, I thought about . . . about leaving them." She squeezed her hands together until her knuckles cracked. "I was going to let them drown." She was glad her mother couldn't see her face. "Don't you understand? I wanted them to drown. Then you wouldn't buy the store and we could move back to Garnet Creek."

Her mother's dim figure loomed solitary and erect and still. Mandy waited for her to repeat her order, but instead she brushed past Mandy and into the flock.

"Let's sit down," she said, pushing a sheep out of the way to make room.

They sat in silence as the night closed down around them. Once a lamb bleated, perhaps for its mother, maybe just for the remembered sanctuary of the barn. Water washed past with a murmuring sound, and the rain still fell, but softly now, as a fine mist. Mandy waited for her mother to speak.

"When you left the store, Mandy, I called to you."

Their painful encounter at the store seemed to have happened years ago, yet Mandy could still recall her mother's awful words against her father.

"I didn't mean what I said, Mandy. I don't hate him." Her voice grew stronger as she continued. "I love him. It's just that I miss him so."

Mandy expelled a long, painful breath. She knew how it felt to miss her father. She'd missed him every day since he'd gone away. She realized that she and her mother had never really talked about him, about missing him.

"Why don't you ever mention him, Mama?"

Her mother fidgeted in the darkness, and when she finally spoke, her voice trembled. "I guess I never really wanted to admit that he's not coming back."

The blunt confession astonished Mandy. Had her mother been hoping, as Ira did, that the army might have made a mistake, that he still might come home?

"He isn't, is he?" Mandy wanted the fact verified once and for all.

"The war has been over for more than a year," her mother said. "If he was alive, he would've come back by now. No, Mandy, he's not coming home."

That was that, Mandy thought, feeling a strange, sad emancipation. Maybe deep down she'd been hoping for a miracle too, but now she knew that all she would ever have of her father was the memories.

"It just scares me when I can't remember his face," Mandy said.

"Sometimes I can't remember either," her mother said. "But we can always remember the love."

Then bright and clear, like the moon coming from behind a cloud, Mandy saw her father's face. He had the same smile, the same dancing eyes she remembered so well. The image wouldn't last, she knew that. But from now on, whenever she missed him, whenever she wanted to remember, she could talk to her mother.

Mandy felt her mother's hand trace her braid down her back. Then her fingers brushed across Mandy's cheek, as soft as a feather. "We'll remember him together," her mother whispered.

Just then, Aunt Bess's voice floated through the night to them. "Are you all right over there?"

They'd both forgotten about her and Ira. They were still waiting for Mandy and her mother to cross back over.

"I'm not going," Mandy murmured just loud enough for her mother to hear.

"Then neither am I," her mother said. She called to Aunt Bess. "We're going to stay here with the sheep."

It was some time before Aunt Bess answered. "Ira and I are going to get help."

Mandy tilted her face to the sky and caught her breath when she saw stars over the rim of the hill. The rain must be about over, although she knew the water would continue to rise for hours yet.

"Mama, maybe we should bring the lambs up to the high ground. They wouldn't have a chance in the water."

"You're right, Mandy. The older sheep are not so likely to panic as the water rises."

One by one, they rounded up the lambs and deposited them in the midst of the flock. At the water's edge, Mandy discovered two lambs huddling close to their mother. When she reached for one of them, they both shied away from her and ended up in the rushing water.

Frantic, Mandy waded in after them. She fought the flood, feeling for the animals, trying to keep her balance in the waist-high current. Finally, she grasped one by its tail. Lucky for that lamb they hadn't got around to cutting off its tail yet. She pulled the lamb to her and held it tight under one arm while she groped for the other one.

Her fingertips grazed the woolly body, but she could not catch hold of it. She combed the water around her long after she knew it was too late. Cradling the single lamb in her arms, she waded out of the water. A few days ago she'd been thinking how good it was that the lambs followed their mothers, but it was that very thing which had put these two in danger. In fact, none of the lambs would be here if they hadn't followed the other sheep. She tried to swallow the ache in her throat, but it wouldn't go away. A picture burned in her mind of the lost lamb trying to swim but being swept under again and again, until . . .

"I lost one of the lambs, Mama."

"Oh, I'm sorry, Mandy. But maybe it will swim to solid ground."

"No, a lamb can't take care of itself," Mandy replied. "It's as helpless as a baby."

Her mother laid a hand on her shoulder. "I don't think you should feel too bad. Most of the sheep are still safe."

"But I didn't want to lose any of them," Mandy murmured. She settled down among the sheep, unable to dismiss the feeling of loss and the overwhelming sense of defeat. She'd been convinced she could save them all.

chapter ❧ seventeen

Several minutes passed before Mandy noticed that the rain had stopped. In the light of the pale, emerging stars she could make out the shape of her mother's face, though her eyes were still hidden in shadows. Mandy hugged her knees to her chest and rested her forehead on them. Her shoulders drooped with a leaden weariness, and she fought off the desire to curl up and go to sleep. Once they got off this island, there'd be plenty of time to sleep. But not yet.

She must have dozed because she jerked when she felt an arm around her shoulders. Her mother's voice was soft, almost a whisper. "Mandy, look. It's morning."

Raising her head from her knees, Mandy saw her mother plainly now in the gray haze that preceded the dawn. Curtains of mist still hung over the water, obscuring their long view, but the sun would soon burn it off. A pink glow in the eastern sky marked its approach.

Minutes after the sun appeared, the mists were gone. Mandy looked around in awe. A vast, chocolate sea covered the valley floor, its surface broken here and there by a partially submerged tree or row of fence posts. Their narrow island, rising only a foot or so above the water, was completely hidden beneath the moving mass of sheep.

When Mandy saw the sheep on the periphery of the flock standing in water up to their bellies, she rose and went down to them. They looked more resigned than afraid, but she waded among them anyway, patting their heads, talking to them under her breath. They had followed their instincts and stayed with the rest of the flock, and it had saved them.

Standing in the water, Mandy circled slowly for a second look at the flooded valley. The hills were vibrant green in the morning sun, and cows grazed undistracted in the fresh-washed, upland pastures. Then Mandy noticed several cars and trucks stopping along the road in front of the schoolhouse. People climbed out of their vehicles, leaving doors ajar, lifting small children up on their shoulders. Some of them began to wave. What a thrilling sight! Mandy raised both arms and waved back.

Her mother called her name, then pointed down the pasture field. A pickup truck bounced toward them, skirting along the edge of the floodwater. As it came closer, Mandy recognized Ned McGuire behind the wheel, and Aunt Bess beside him. The truck rolled to a halt at the point closest to the island.

Mandy saw Ira slide out of the back, then gaped when Dean appeared, followed by Curtis and his friend, Calhoun. Aunt Bess had brought all kinds of help.

The boys stood there staring across the water, but as Ned walked to the back of the truck, they scurried after him. They wrestled the flat-bottomed boat off the truck and into the water, then locked the oars in place. For a moment they gathered around it, talking in voices too low for Mandy to hear.

Finally Ned and Dean climbed in the boat and shoved off toward the island. Though the current tried to carry them downstream, Ned's strong strokes brought them in among the sheep. Dean jumped into the water and held the boat steady while Ned stepped out. The man smiled at Mandy and her mother. "We would've been here sooner, but I had to go up to the lake and get my boat," he said.

Mandy's mother pushed through the sheep. "We're sure glad to see you, Ned."

"We might as well get started," he said. "We can take you two first, before we start ferrying the sheep over."

Mandy looked at her mother and shook her

head. "We'll go later," her mother told Ned. Then she pointed to the sheep standing in water. "These ought to go first."

Ned nodded, picked up a ewe and set her in the bottom of the boat. She looked wild-eyed as she swayed to keep her balance in the unsteady craft. While Ned and Dean loaded the boat, Mandy and her mother tried to quiet the frightened animals with gentle pats and soothing words. When the boat was full, Ned climbed in and settled at the oars. Kneeling among the sheep with a lamb under each arm, Dean grinned at Mandy as the boat pulled away.

The crossing took only a couple of minutes and the sheep were soon on solid ground. The boat returned to the island and was quickly loaded, then set off again. Only two lambs were taken on each trip so that Dean could hold on to them and keep them from jumping out of the boat. Mandy saw one do just that as the boat neared the shore where Aunt Bess and the boys waited. Somehow, the lamb got away from Dean and plunged over the side. It went under and immediately bobbed to the surface again beside the boat. Dean, still clinging to the other lamb, couldn't reach the one in the water, but Curtis jumped to the rescue. He waded out, seized the lamb by its woolly neck, and carried it ashore in his arms.

After four trips, sheep still covered the narrow island, but there were none left standing in the water. With every load that made its way safely into Aunt Bess's care, Mandy's spirits felt a little lighter. Finally there were only ten animals left on the island, six ewes and four lambs. Curtis had relieved Ned at the oars, and watching him and Dean working side by side, Mandy couldn't help but smile. Maybe they'd be friends by the time this was all over.

"You can go with this load, Mama. I'll come over with the rest."

Her mother nodded, seeming to understand Mandy's need to stay until the last sheep was off the island. Dean, remaining with Mandy, shoved the boat out into the current.

"Were you over here all night?" he asked her.

"Yes, but during the night Mama came over and stayed with me. What were you doing at Aunt Bess's?"

"The storm woke me and I got to worrying about the sheep, so at first light I headed out to see about them. Over the high ground," he added, pointing to the hill that Mandy had climbed so many times in the past weeks. "Just as I got to the farm, Ned pulled in with Curtis and Calhoun. He'd picked them up on the road."

They were quiet for several moments, watching the unloading on the other shore.

"Were any of the sheep . . . uh, lost?" Dean asked. "I mean, I haven't seen Molly."

"One lamb, I know for sure. I almost had it, but I couldn't hold on. Molly might be with the ones I took back to the barn last night," she added.

"I hope so." Dean's eyes softened as he gazed at Mandy. "You were brave to stay over here with them all night."

"Brave!" Mandy shook her head. She knew better than that. When she'd waded over to the island, she'd simply been trying to get rid of her guilt. It had been bigger and heavier than her fear of the flood.

Curtis rowed back alone for the final load. Mandy waited until the boys and the sheep were aboard, then she pushed the boat off and hopped in. Sitting in the stern seat, she found herself opposite a red-faced Curtis. He looked at her only once, then stared down at his muddy boots, his arms pulling with long, powerful strokes. Mandy wasn't really mad at him anymore. In fact, she was grateful for his help with the sheep. But she wasn't quite ready to be friends yet.

When the boat ground to a stop and the boys began unloading the last animals, a roaring sound reverberated from the surrounding hills. The crowd over by the schoolhouse had begun cheering, waving, honking their horns in rousing celebration of the rescue. It was several minutes before the noise died away, and the satisfied observers began to depart.

As Mandy gazed at the distant crowd, she felt a hand on her shoulder. She turned and looked into Aunt Bess's tired face.

"You shouldn't have left the barn last night, Mandy."

"I know," Mandy replied, feeling sorry for all the worry she'd caused.

"I'm proud of you just the same," Aunt Bess said. Then she reached over and brushed a wet strand of hair from Mandy's eyes. Despite her knobby fingers, it was a gentle caress.

A mixture of surprise and pleasure warmed Mandy as she watched Aunt Bess turn and walk to the truck. Thinking of last night's darkness and danger, Mandy never would have imagined so many good things could come out of the storm.

With the boat secured in the truck, Ned turned the vehicle and headed for the farm, taking the two women with him. Ira jumped in the back, but the other boys stayed with Mandy and the sheep.

For a moment, Mandy gazed back at the tiny, trampled patch of earth that had been their life raft in the storm. There was no use thinking about what might have happened. All that mattered was that she and her mother and the sheep were safe.

Most of the sheep. They wouldn't know for sure how many were missing until they got back to the barn.

Curtis and Calhoun walked in front of the flock, leaving Mandy and Dean to mingle with the stragglers. As the sun warmed them, Mandy's wet clothes began to itch, and she rubbed and scratched all the way to the barn.

By the time she and Dean followed the last of the sheep into the barn, the feed troughs had already been filled with corn and oats. Leaning against a feed bin, Mandy watched Aunt Bess counting the animals.

"There are three missing," she said at last. "Two grown sheep and a lamb."

"The lamb got swept away last night," Mandy told her.

"It's a miracle more weren't lost," Aunt Bess said. "Sheep are such followers."

Mandy wondered at Aunt Bess's coldhearted attitude toward the sheep. She didn't even seem upset about the ones she'd lost. Maybe it was better that way, better not to make them so important that they had to have names. But Mandy recalled the moment last night when she'd discovered Mildred. It had been like finding an old friend in a crowd of strangers.

She noticed Dean moving among the sheep and knew he was searching for Molly. He pushed lambs and yearlings out of his way to get a closer look at the ewes. Finally, his troubled gaze found Mandy and he shook his head. Weariness, like a giant wave, washed over Mandy.

"What we all need is a good breakfast," Aunt Bess announced from the open barn door. "If you boys will bring in some wood, I'll get a fire going. I've got enough bacon and eggs for everybody."

"You got any cinnamon rolls, Aunt Bess?" Ira asked.

"We'll see," she replied, heading for the house.

Moments later, Mandy heard Aunt Bess give a snort of surprise as she stopped short and stared down the lane. Mandy turned and looked too, and could hardly believe what she saw. June came striding toward them, eyes glowing, carrying a lamb in her arms.

"I found it caught in some brush along the lane," she said to Aunt Bess. "I guess it belongs to you."

"I guess it does," Aunt Bess said, taking the bewildered animal and handing it to Mandy.

There was a painful swelling in Mandy's chest. Somehow the lamb she'd lost in last night's darkness had survived the flood. Cradled in her arms, it was as frayed and limp as an old rope. You fought a good fight, Mandy silently praised it, good enough to stay alive.

While June talked with Aunt Bess, Dean and Ira followed Mandy inside and watched her set the lamb in with the rest of the sheep. The other lambs were already asleep, and most of the grown sheep too. Several ewes raised their heads when the rescued lamb bleated, and one anxious ewe came to investigate. Coming together, she and the lamb touched noses in recognition, then the lamb went looking for milk.

Mandy saw Mildred coming toward her and held out her hand. Once the ewe had examined it and found it empty, she gazed up at Mandy with those solemn, questioning eyes.

"She's glad to be home," Dean said.

Mandy saw Dean's gaze move over the resting flock. No doubt he was thinking of Molly. But even if Molly was still here, he didn't have the money to buy her. He wouldn't have enough money for months, and maybe not then either, if his father found it again.

Suddenly Mandy knew what she must do. The money her father had sent her wouldn't be needed now. In saving the lambs, Mandy had finally accepted the fact that they would be buying the store instead of the Fulton place. So if she couldn't use the money to get her own dream, she could use it to help Dean get his. She felt only a soft twinge of regret as she turned to face him.

"I have some money my father sent to me," she began. "I want to loan it to you so you can buy a ewe." She watched the changing expressions on Dean's face; first surprise, then a flicker of hope, then a sober, sad calm.

"I couldn't . . ." he murmured, shaking his head.

"Why not?" Mandy asked, ready to reject every one of his reasons for refusing the money.

Just then, Ira spoke up. "Mandy, I thought that money was for the Fulton . . ."

Mandy cut him off. "We're going to live in Parrish Grove from now on." She turned to Dean. "I've been saving the money for a dream, and that's what it should be used for." She could almost feel Dean's yearning.

"I don't know when I could pay it back," he said at last. "There's the map money . . ."

"I can wait," Mandy said. Her mother still might want to borrow the money, but she would worry about that later.

"And your Aunt Bess might not want to sell any sheep since she lost those in the flood."

"She'll sell," Mandy said with a knowing smile, recalling Aunt Bess's remarks about Dean and the ewe.

"You might need the money."

"There's nothing I need," Mandy said. I don't even need the Fulton place anymore, she thought. At that moment, she had the odd sensation of a weight being lifted from her shoulders.

Dean stood, hands in his pockets, staring at the hay-strewn floor. He bent and picked up a single stalk of hay, brushed it off and clamped it between his teeth. Then he looked over at Mandy. Surrender was there in his wide smile and flashing eyes, along with a trembling, almost uncontainable joy.

"Good," Mandy said. "There's only one condition. Nobody's to know where you got the money, not even Aunt Bess." When Dean nodded agreement, Mandy turned to Ira. "Don't you dare tell anyone about it either."

"Are you threatening me?" Ira asked, scowling at her.

"That's exactly what I'm doing," she said. "And you'd better do as I say this time." Ira just grinned at her and scampered out the barn door.

June was leaning against a fence post, studying the flooded valley, as Mandy and Dean stepped outside.

"We were going to make paper flowers today," she said to Mandy. "Remember?"

Mandy smiled at her and nodded, though she had forgotten about it in the turmoil of the night.

"I'd better come back some other time. Your mother said you were up all night. Maybe tomorrow."

"Tomorrow probably would be better," Mandy said. "But you have to stay for breakfast."

June nodded and they headed for the house. As they were passing the porch, the front door rattled, then swung open, and a moment later Aunt Bess appeared in the doorway.

"June, I'm expecting you to stay for breakfast." Her eyes narrowed as they shifted to Mandy. It must have been the puzzlement on Mandy's face that prompted her to add, "I came across the front door key yesterday." Without waiting for a response from any of them, she turned back inside and shut the door.

Mandy smiled to herself as they continued on to the back door. She wouldn't be fooled anymore by Aunt Bess's gruff, bossy manner. There was no doubt in Mandy's mind that Aunt Bess had been searching for that lost door key for weeks.

As they entered the big kitchen, Mandy breathed in the delicious aroma of frying bacon. It had been a long time since her last meal. She saw Curtis and Calhoun noisily trying to make room for all the necessary chairs around the table. Ira had already claimed a seat for himself.

Mandy was splashing water on her face when she felt a hand on her wet, frazzled braid. Her mother, hair combed, wearing dry clothes, said, "If you hurry, Mandy, you'll have time to change before we eat."

Mandy nodded and headed for the stairs. Once dry and comfortable again, she paused to look at herself in the mirror. Her eyes, as deeply brown as her father's, stared back at her. Despite the fatigue and the almost overwhelming desire to sleep, she felt strangely elated. It was as if the new day had brought her a new life.

She opened her dresser drawer, pulled out six of the five-dollar bills and slipped them into her pocket. Maybe this was the beginning of a new life for Dean too.